I0549263

SECRETS

Sybil Norcroft Book Three

Carl Douglass

Neurosurgeon Turned Author Writes with Gripping Realism

PO Box 221974 Anchorage, Alaska 99522-1974
books@publicationconsultants.com—www.publicationconsultants.com

ISBN 978-1-59433-483-2
eISBN 978-1-59433-484-9
Library of Congress Catalog Card Number: 2014910364

Manufactured in the United States of America.

Dedication

To my family

Disclaimer

All of the six novellas in the Sybil Series are works of fiction and should not be construed as representing real persons, places, or events. Some names of real persons and places appear but only for the purpose of creating a setting in the real world or as a mention of historical circumstances. None of the real people or the real places were actually involved in the fictional portrayals found in these short books. All of the events described were created from the author's imagination.

Dedication

To my family

Books By Carl Douglass

Heaven and Hell
Garven Wilsonhulme takes on all comers in the jungle of modern competition Saga of a Neurosurgeon Series, Book Three

The Long Climb
Young M.D., Garven Wilsonhulme, engaged in a social poker game of winner takes all Saga of a Neurosurgeon Series, Book Four

ACADEMIA: The Law of the Jungle
Surgeon in training, Garven Wilsonhulme, fang-and-claw competition for glory Saga of a Neurosurgeon Series, Book Five

The Vulture and the Phoenix
Neurosurgeon, Garven Wilsonhulme, the final great fight Saga of a Neurosurgeon Series, Book Six

Finders Keepers, Losers Weep
A Novel of Innocence Betrayed and the Search for Restitution

Gog and Magog
Yawm al-Qiyamah, Yawm al-Din The Day of Judgment

Sheep Dog and the Wolf
A Story of Terrorism and Response, and the Sheep Dogs Who Protect

Though They Come from the Ends of the Earth
A Novel of the Iran Nuclear Weapons Interdiction Project Book One of the Trojan Horse in the Belly of the Beast Trilogy

Dancing with the Devil
A Novel of the Iran Nuclear Weapons Interdiction Project Book Two of the Trojan Horse in the Belly of the Beast Trilogy

The Trojan Horse in the Belly of the Beast
A Novel of the Iran Nuclear Weapons Interdiction Project Book Three of the Trojan Horse in the Belly of the Beast Trilogy

The End of the Beginning
Sybil Norcroft Book One

Uncharted Country, Uncertain Future
Sybil Norcroft Book Two

Secrets
Sybil Norcroft Book Three

Secrets and Scandals
Sybil Norcroft Book Four

Decisions
Sybil Norcroft Book Five

Running with the Big Dogs
Sybil Norcroft Book Six

NONFICTION

On Evolution
The Origin of Selection, Order, Progression, and Diversity
Out of print

Something About Religion
Out of print

Chapter One

S ybil sat uncomfortably on a utilitarian chair. She had a good idea of what was going to go on, and had no explicit fear; but the Spartan room was discomfiting. She was in the J. Edgar Hoover Federal Bureau of Investigation building, after all.

"*This is a positive thing, just tell the truth; after all you are just here to be sure that you aren't a monster undeserving of the great honor for which the president has recommended you,*" she told herself several times. "*And, yes, there is that secret part—two lie detector tests for the price of one.*"

She seemed to get less sure of herself every time she repeated her litany. She decided to do her self-relaxation exercises and closed her eyes; so, her mind could take her somewhere else. She went back to a point a year ago when she was just a very successful neurosurgeon going about her satisfying practice; back to the time before she had been sued again for malpractice; back to that idyllic era before she had been indicted and tried for first degree murder and grand larceny. And, yes, before she had been thrust into the klieg-light glare of national prominence—fame or notoriety; she was unable to be sure she could tell the difference any longer.

Two serious men entered the room.

"Good morning, Dr. Norcroft. I hope you are feeling well and relaxed this morning," the older of the two said by way of greeting.

"Good morning, gentlemen," Sybil responded.

She noted that neither of the two ventured his name, the agency for which he worked, or his purpose.

The younger man, dressed in his Class-A uniform—blue serge suit, white shirt, plain maroon tie, black wing-tip shoes from Brooks Brothers—did not greet nor speak to Dr. Norcroft. He sat at a small table and prepared recording materials.

The older of the two was twice the age of the younger man, had a care-worn nearly expressionless face, and a nearly bald head sprouting patches of grey-white hair that had once been light brown. He wore an older version of the blue-serge suit—out-of-style three button jacket, pleated pants with cuffs, button-down white shirt with a bow tie, black suspenders, and highly polished black wing-tips as well-cared-for as the younger man's but showing age along their seams.

"Dr. Norcroft, we are here to administer a polygraph test, or, as it is known popularly, a lie-detector test," said the older of the two agents, "have you ever had a polygraph?"

"No, Sir."

"All right, Doctor. Your part is simple in that test. When I ask you a question, you answer yes or no and do not amplify. Relax and tell the truth. We are not here to make judgments about the content of the information we gather from you, but our job is to come to a conclusion about whether or not you have lied to us. Everyone lies and does so frequently, often not even realizing that what they are saying is a lie. Everyone has secrets. Our interests lie in determining whether you are lying about anything we consider to be substantive and whether, over all, you are a truthful person or not. We do not make decisions about the fact that you either lie or tell the truth. That is for a higher authority. Do you understand me so far?"

"I do."

"Are you ready?"

"As I will ever be, I guess."

"Everything is going to be recorded, and a transcript printed. It will be 'eyes and ears only' for a handful of people who need to know including the president and a few of his close associates and to any senior officer of a federal agency who requests information about this examination and has the required top-secret clearance. Do you understand that part of what will happen today?"

"Yes."

"I have clearance to tell you a couple of things you need to know. First, should you agree to a contract and are accepted for employment with an intelligence agency, you may lie upon occasion, may even be ordered to do so; but you must never lie in even the most trivial instance today or ever to your superiors—those who know about and handle your mission. Your polygraph interview today will never identify you by name, but will be given a number and will enter into the file that will be kept on you in accordance with the National Secrets Act. That understood?"

"Yes, Sir," Sybil answered.

"At the risk of repeating myself, are you ready?"

Sybil was getting weary of the preliminaries and legalistic approach to everything federal she had thus far and contact with.

"I am," she said working to keep a note of irritation out of her voice and off her face.

"*He is just doing his job,*" she whispered inwardly, not for the last time during the polygraph experience.

"For now, my co-worker and I will query you about your activities and experiences in an interview format; and you are directed to give a narrative answer at this point in time. Tell me about your early life and educational background briefly."

Sybil told him—them. It took forty minutes.

The older man turned to the younger one, "Your turn."

The younger of the two men said, "Doctor, tell us something about your life as a surgeon, please."

Sybil told him about her internship and residency, about the research that led to her getting a Ph.D. in addition to her M.D., and the sexism she had had to cope with before finally getting the plum appointment on the staff of Joseph Nobel Memorial Hospital in Los Angeles, and then watching her career take wings. She told him about being subjected to less than equal respect at the hospital and then went into a lengthy review of her medical malpractice defense history—having been sued nine times in eleven years by the same plaintiff's attorney.

The older man took the next set of questions.

"You owned a horse breeding ranch, is that correct?"

"Yes, it is."

"Did you employ illegal immigrants at any time?"

"Briefly. Later on, they all were granted amnesty by President Bush and now hold green cards and are progressing towards citizenship."

The young man took notes during which time there was quiet in the room.

"Did you ever ask your Mexican workers to do anything illegal?"

Sybil paused before answering, "No," she said.

"You did not respond as quickly as you usually do to that question. Do you need to amplify your answer?"

"Not really, I had to weigh in my mind whether anything illegal was done, and I came to the conclusion that none had."

"Tell us about your activities outside work."

Sybil explained her extra-curricular involvement with LGPT and feminist organizations, her serious and time-consuming activities with the senior officers of neurosurgical groups and foundations.

The older agent took his turn, "Tell us about your work for the government and the CDC in particular during the recent Marburg virus epidemic, please."

It took her more than half an hour to go through the long story. She was as succinct as possible but took pains to include necessary details from beginning to end. She told the two men about becoming the senior medical consultant for Wolf News Channel and being thrust into a high-profile effort to find and capture Jean-Pierre Alain Pourciau, a senior officer of the Fabrique Pharmaceutique DRC in the Congo. The man was a human-trafficker, an enslaver of young pygmy girls—most of whom were forced into sexual servitude. What he did that attracted the attention of U.S. intelligence services, the FBI, the CDC, Wolf News, and the president, she told him, was to act in concert with al Qaeda to produce and to weaponize strains of the extraordinarily virulent Marburg virus which caused a nearly always fatal hemorrhagic fever illness. She carefully spoke of her role in tracking down and capturing Pourciau, but only after he had started a major epidemic in the United States that also spread abroad.

"I understand that you ended up adopting one of the unfortunate little girls from the Congo, is that right?"

"That's true."

"Tell us about your murder case. Please do not spare the details," the tired older man asked.

She knew the question was coming, but she had to take a deep breath to dredge the painful era in her life back up again.

"I received my tenth 'intent-to-sue letter from my old nemesis, attorney Paul Devon Bel Gedde, around Christmas time about two years ago. That attorney and I had words at a fund-raiser in LA, and I got angry and said some things I now wish I could take back. A few days later, Mr. Bel Geddes was murdered—shot in the back of the head with a shotgun—during a robbery in his home in Bel Aire. Because of our long and unfriendly history, I became a suspect in that murder. I was finally indicted and brought to trial on first degree murder and grand larceny charges."

"I understand that your trial was one of the most sensational in the history of Los Angeles which has certainly seen more than its share of attention grabbing trial events. Tell us about the trial."

Sybil took her time and gave a remarkably detailed rendition of the trial demonstrating her firm grasp of legal and medical issues, trial proceedings, and the circumstances surrounding her being found not guilty and being given a full positive treatment by the judge, the jury, and the news media.

"You made some friends in law enforcement during the trial, Dr. Norcroft. Isn't that so?"

"I did," she said and went on to tell about her involvement with Detective Lieutenant Anson Burger, his partner, Griselda Müller, better known as "Grizzly", a pair of private investigators, Drew Knox and Amber Littlefeather, and FBI Special Agent Grant Walsh.

She described them as being remarkably determined and able investigators who broke the case wide open during her trial and led to her being fully exonerated almost as the jury foreperson was about to hand over a guilty verdict to the judge in the case.

Chapter Two

"What's this business about you wanting to do your bit for the country in the War On Terrorism?" the young agent asked and glanced at his note pad. "I think your exact words to confidants were that you wanted to make some sort of a 'small contribution'."

"I don't know, maybe it's just a mid-life crisis; but yes, I have been frustrated in general with the monstrous things the terrorists do; and I wanted to be part of the effort to thwart them. I don't fancy myself a Jane Bond type, but my intuition is that there are people behind the scenes—even way behind—that do a lot. I guess—if the truth be known—that was my secret fantasy. Learning first-hand about the dreadful al Qaeda plan to infect the world with a pestilence of biblical proportions was the final trigger."

The older agent then commented, "It has been suggested to us that you have perhaps been offered a not great paying, hazardous, uncomfortable, and unsung hero type job that just might make a difference? Anything to that?"

"Something," she bantered, not at all sure that these two men had the necessary clearance to learn what the president and the agency had proposed.

"Good answer," the agent said, "we'll let it go at that."

"I think we've learned enough from our interview for the time being, Dr. Norcroft. We think it is time to conduct the formal scientific polygraph test. After that, the people who sent you to us can let you know about your standing for an award and can then talk more definitively with you about a contract."

He got up abruptly and stretched out. He invited Sybil and the younger agent to do the same thing before starting the next phase of her vetting. The two special agents of the FBI motioned for Sybil to follow them. They went to a room with an obvious one-way mirror and motioned for Sybil to sit. She took the seat proffered—one with an obvious sensor pad on the seat—and sat facing the colorless functionary across a small table which was covered with medical appearing paraphernalia.

The younger agent seated in the chair opposite to Sybil said, "Please take off your shoes."

Sybil did. The agent then placed a mirror next to Sybil's left foot and proceeded to affix a sphyngmanometer to her right arm, a plethsmygraph band around her chest—apologizing for the slight contact with her thorax—electrodermal galvanic skin response electrode patches on her right hand, and had her unbutton her blouse so he could place ECG leads on her chest. He wheeled a computer screen up to the table so that Sybil faced it directly, then he placed a P300 wave analysis electrode headband on her forehead. Lastly, the young man placed a PSE machine next to Sybil's mouth—a psychological stress evaluator for voice stress analysis.

The younger man did not speak again until after his set-up was complete, then he repeated the older man's instructions and admonitions, "You are about to take a polygraph or lie detector test. I direct you to tell the truth to every question asked since the polygraph equipment will detect every lie by showing even the slightest stress. You cannot alter your responses in any way to trick the machine since your responses are automatic. The machine is sensitive to all of the fight, flight, and freeze mechanisms of human physiology. My associate will ask a series of questions—some of which may be repetitive—in order to verify any responses that indicate falsification on your part. He is a trained and qualified expert and has done thousands of these tests. We will be aware of any effort on your part to lie or to evade the truth.

"You have the right to refuse to take the polygraph test; but if you do, you will probably not receive your award nor will you receive a contract from the U.S. government. The polygraph test is not the sole determiner of whether these things you apparently desire will come to you; but, in all probability, you cannot fail your polygraph and be successful. If you elect to proceed, you will be given questions that deal with your life's experience, any criminal record you may have, your employment record, medical information, and your intentions. By agreeing to proceed, you are agreeing to allow the information from the test and from the forms you filled out to be passed on to the president and to any agency he deems necessary. Have you any questions?"

"No."

"Do you wish to proceed?" he asked again.

"Yes."

"Hereafter, answer only yes or no. Answer truthfully, and keep your mouth open and your hands on the table at all times between answers."

Sybil nodded her understanding and agreement.

"Did you sleep more than six hours last night?"

"Yes."

"Did you eat breakfast this morning?"

"Yes."

"Have you had corrective eye surgery?"

"No."

His numerous preliminary questions dealt with known truths, facts about Sybil's life that she had placed on the forms she had filled out and which had all been covered in the interview wherein she gave narrative answers. The questions included topics related to her general honesty, suitability, and integrity. He asked about Sybil's criminal record—nonexistent except for the murder charge for which she had been acquitted and exonerated—her general propensity to lie, whether she had ever lied for any reason, any drug use, whether she had ever committed and gotten away with arson, murder, assault, sexual exposure, sex with a minor as an adult, forgery, or had any weapons violations not previously recorded. Did Sybil steal, take credit for work done by others, cheat at cards, ever do anything she was ashamed of, withhold necessary information in an investigation, or had she ever done anything for which she could have been fired or prosecuted? Sybil paused on a few of them, but did try and tell the truth as best she could knowing that some of her answers required more than a simple 'yes' or 'no'.

Then the technician got to the nitty-gritty questions.

"Do you know anyone who is involved in espionage or sabotage against the United States?"

"No."

"Have you ever copied or removed classified material without permission?"

"No."

"Have you ever made unreported visits to foreign countries or embassies?"

"No."

"Have you ever been approached, trained by, made plans with, or been compensated by any person involved in espionage or sabotage against the United States?"

"No."

He went through a long list of closely related questions about Sybil's possible contacts with organized criminals who associated with terrorists, any unauthorized contacts that could pose a threat to the country, any compromising sexual and pornographic proclivities, and did Sybil have any belief in a religion or philosophy or group that espoused injury to the country. Her answers were all negative.

"That is all," the technician said and dismantled the equipment from her.

The interrogators left the room and Special Agent Grant Walsh—whom she knew from the Marburg virus epidemic effort—came in. He had obviously been watching from behind the one-way mirror—for how long, she did not know. That had to be one of the world's most boring jobs, Sybil thought. They walked down the stairs to the conference room where they got lunch. She suddenly realized that she was starved. Half way through the meal, they were joined by Ed Simonsen, the CIA agent with whom she had also worked during the Marburg scare.

"Old home week," Sybil quipped.

Chapter Three

Sybil Norcroft and her husband, Charles Daniels, received a formal invitation to a black-tie welcoming event in the East Room of the White House prior to being driven in presidential limousines to the Kennedy Center for the 38th annual Presidential Medal of Freedom Awards. Sybil was one of 17 recipients for 2015 and 534 since the award was created by President John F. Kennedy 50+ years previously. Led by Wolf News, Sybil's image in the media became better known than the pope, the author of *Fifty Shades of Grey*—the world's best-selling novel—or the sitting vice-president. Leading up to the event, Sybil met with President Willets one-on-one twice, and with the group of recipients three times. She appeared on Wolf News as a celebrity as opposed to her professional role as the senior medical consultant 24 times and on WWN, ABC, CBS, and NBC—Wolf's competitors—three times each. David Kilcannon, vice-president of Wolf News production, and Sybil met with a ghost writer, Erik Søren Nordstrom, to get work going on a book that told of her life, career, and adventures. There was no intention to make the book objective, but Sybil refused to permit hyperbole beyond a reasonable point or outright falsehoods. The nearest she came to agreeing to a false statement was when she announced the publication of her as yet unwritten non-fiction book—with its expected launch date of December 15—just in time for the Christmas rush.

She was tired from the whole whirlwind of hype surrounding her, the thrice daily speeches, and the myriad of public appearances, which had been orchestrated by the Wolf News publicity department. Charles was tired *of* what he considered to be a huge phony business. He restrained himself from telling Sybil what he really thought—that the whole circus was beneath her dignity, and she should just let the important award speak for itself.

President Parker Conrad Willets—his usual tall, greying, handsome, self—was effusive with his praise for all of the recipients. Wolf News made a full good faith effort to make sure that the East Room ceremony and the actual award ceremony at the Kennedy Center were fully videoed—82% of the coverage being centered on Sybil—and purchased multi-channel advertising time to tout their golden girl. The photogenic, fetching, and brilliant raconteur and dramatic professional persona of Sybil was fast becoming a household fixture. Not many Americans could tell you the names of even two of the other award recipients. She was wearing a modest full length form fitting black Vera Wang evening gown and a simple diamond pendant. Because she was 15 years younger and light years more beautiful that the next awardee, it seemed even to the most casual observer to be Sybil's night to shine.

The awards were presented in alphabetical order with the president placing the circular, gold, star-emblazoned medals on a blue ribbon around the recipients' necks. Sybil was the twelfth awardee to be called up to the podium to receive her medal. Each of the awardees in his or her turn was heralded by a brief description in glowing terms about his or her life and accomplishments. There was a notable difference in what the president had to say about Sybil. His comments would have led one to presume that Dr. Norcroft was more than an esteemed and worthy individual, but also almost something of a colleague of the president's. She was perceptive enough to recognize the difference and intelligent enough to tuck a little note of concern into the back of her mind—"*what is all of that about?*"

The president's laudatory comments about Sybil were fairly brief. He looked away from his printed notes to deliver the final paragraph.

"Finally, my fellow Americans, friends, family and esteemed guests, let me say this of Dr. Norcroft: She is a brave, passionate American, a humanitarian, a brilliant scholar, and an agent of change who will continue to contribute to the best our society can produce. I predict that she will soon have an official role in government that will assist her in her ability to make that contribution."

Not everyone agreed with the president's laudatory comments about Dr. Norcroft. In private, Raza Patel—the WWN senior medical consultant—described her to friends as a solipsist possessing extreme ego centrism. His ratings plummeted when Wolf News was able to air the WWN star's comments verbatim due to the failure of technicians to turn off all microphones—a not uncommon error usually committed by politicians. An unnamed source was quoted on MSNBC as saying that Dr. Norcroft claimed credit for the humanitarian effort to control the Marburg virus epidemic that should have gone to the Democratic senator from Maryland who sponsored the Senate bill which appropriated funds for the effort. Tea Party critics from Florida accused the Presidential Medal of Freedom recipient of being just another big-government toady.

Sybil had three days of rest during which time her past and more recent accomplishments and exploits were kept alive on the Wolf News Channel by re-airing archive material which had been filmed by her photographer and friend, Doug Mason, and edited by the redoubtable and indefatigable Edith Headman. She returned to work to a standing ovation by her fellow workers and ingratiated herself to them by blushing to a crimson complexion.

David Kilcannon, Vice-President of Wolf News production, met her after she walked around shaking everyone else's hands and receiving their expressions of fulsome praise and genuine affection.

"Well, Sybil, you seem to have reached the pinnacle. To get right to the point, we need to keep you relevant."

"How do we do that, David? It seems like the Medal of Freedom award will be hard to top or even equal."

"Certainly, and we shouldn't even try. We can shift your image to the elder-statesperson image that used to be held by Raza Patel over at that other station—what's its name?"

Both laughed at the facetious slighting reference to WWN, which was the world's premier news channel irrespective of Sybil's relatively recent meteoric rise on the Wolf News Channel.

"Barbara Welhelme, the editorial staff, and I have been discussing some options. We all agree that you need a new pertinent and timely project befitting the "elder-statesperson" persona. What do you think about Wolf beginning a series on trauma in the United States, especially among children? We can highlight the profound impact childhood trauma has in the blighted inner cities. What do you think about that, Sybil?"

"I relish the opportunity. I suggest that we do what almost amounts to a mini-series, the last of which would be on suicide. We can cover the subject in general, focus a lot of attention on children, bring in survivors, psychologists, ER doctors, and provide our audience with good, evidence-based recommendations for prevention. And, we need to go during prime time on Sundays."

"We didn't think it through that well, Sybil. Of course, that is the way to go. We are overjoyed at having your brains working for our channel. Maybe one day we will get a bigger market share than WWN, who knows?"

The first hour-long show opened with a disclaimer suggesting that those whose sensitivities would be offended by graphic images should consider not watching the show and that parents should make wise choices about whether or not to permit their children to watch. Every news channel in the world knew that such an announcement would guarantee a 38% increase in viewership. Immediately after the disclaimer, a montage of sports, vehicular, workplace, and crime related images of trauma flashed in vivid red and orange hues accompanied by a cacophony of sirens, screams, weeping, and the voices of law enforcement officers, firemen, EMS personnel, doctors, and nurses. Then, the images were removed. During a moment of silence, spotlights centered on a loan figure seated in the middle of the studio stage; and Sybil Norcroft, M.D., Ph.D., F.A.C.S. began to speak quietly.

"My friends, every year in the United States, trauma accounts for 42 million emergency department visits and over two million admissions to our nation's hospitals and 30% of all life-years lost in our country. Cancer, heart disease, and HIV are certainly serious threats to the health of our people; but to put this matter of trauma into perspective, we should all understand that the impact on years of life lost from trauma is equal to or greater than all those lost to cancer, heart disease, and HIV combined. Trauma affects all ages in our country, especially in the young and among our seniors. Trauma ranks number one for the age group one to forty-four—a staggering almost 50% of all deaths in this age range. Across all age groups, trauma is the third leading cause of death. The economic burden is truly staggering—$406 billion a year, once you factor in both health care costs and lost productivity.

"Think about what that means. In the past two decades, improvement in the death rates of those three disease entities has not improved to any great degree; and many deaths from trauma could be prevented with proper attention to safety measures. 450,000 burn injuries require medical attention every year. One-third of older adults experience a fall each year with well over eight million people treated in emergency departments for nonfatal injuries related to falls; 2.5 million of these were people aged over 65 years, and nearly 600,000 of those were hospitalized at a dreadful financial cost to say nothing about the degree of individual and family suffering. A considerable number of those accidents were preventable.

"The Center for Disease Control—the CDC, as it is better known—is the organization with which I worked during the recent terroristic Marburg virus epidemic. The CDC is working to raise awareness about access to and locations of trauma centers in the United States so that people can live to their fullest potential, despite even severe injuries they may experience. You may not be aware that while most injuries can be treated at a local emergency department; if you are severely injured, getting care at a Level I trauma center can lower your risk of death by 25%. We the People need to be willing to fund—yes, through that nasty word, "taxes"—the creation of more such centers and to support the creation of a significant number of new highly trained trauma treatment experts.

"We can dramatically lower those dreadful traumatic injury statistics by demanding better firearms training and control, more stringent on-the-job safety measures and supervision, better sports equipment—such as football helmets, eye protectors, and neck braces—and safety awareness education in our schools from pre-school to the end of college. Parents can learn such simple precautions as avoiding lifting a baby or a toddler up by one arm or jerking on the arm of a young child. Every year too many children use the use of an arm because of unthinking arm injury inflicted by a well-meaning parent or family member, for example.

"Tonight and for the next six weeks, we will present hour long programs to enlighten you and to convince you about the seriousness of trauma for our country and its citizens. Each of these programs will be uninterrupted by commercials until the end of the program. We have carefully chosen which companies' products will be appropriate for such important studies, and we urge you to support those companies which make this series possible."

Wolf News's ratings soared nearly 25 points above WWN and eclipsed ABC, NBC, and CBS during the hour before, the hour of, and the hour after Sybil's programs. She was awarded an Alfred I. duPont-Columbia University Award which honors excellence in broadcast and digital journalism. The award is comparable to the Pulitzer Prize for print journalism and an Emmy for the best educational series for 2015. The programs were broadcast globally to an enthusiastic world-wide audience. That prompted President Willets to invite Sybil to another one-on-one meeting in the Oval Office.

"Dr. Norcroft," he said, as soon as she was shown into the world's most important room, "you continue to amaze me. Whatever the world lost when you stopped doing surgery, it gained exponentially from your efforts at Wolf News. The trauma series was absolutely outstanding. I admit to having an ulterior motive related to your international success. You probably remember during one of our meetings some months ago when I alluded to wanting to have another meeting with you, I trust?"

"I do."

"Well, this is it. Members of my administration, especially the intelligence services, are well aware of your contributions to the health and well-being of the citizens of the world. In addition, it did not go unnoticed that you acted in the capacity of an intelligence agent during the efforts to capture and to bring to justice the monsters who perpetrated the Marburg virus epidemic. That was important, but I am sure you recognize that it was just one small step in our efforts to get ahead of al Qaeda and other terrorist organizations. We want you to help your country with another such step."

"I would be happy to be of service, Mr. President."

"I was sure you would. This service would have to be a strictly secret one, and not one that would ever see the light of day, let alone become known to the public through your association with Wolf News. I want you to accept an offer to be a contract officer in the Central Intelligence Agency. I am sure you remember Ed Simonsen. He would be your handler, your immediate superior officer. Is that something you would consider? Your high profile would blend nicely with several missions that we wish to accomplish."

"I will be glad to help. What happens next?"

"I like that practical attitude, Dr. Norcroft. I expected that would be your answer. So much so that I have invited Agent Simonsen and the DDCIA [Deputy Director of the CIA], Andrew Dillon, to join us. We can get down to the nuts and bolts of the arrangement between you and the agency."

"Sounds good, I'm ready."

Sybil's heart was racing at the thought of becoming a spy. It was almost impossible to be blasé about such a prospect. Erin Novak, the president's secretary, ushered the two men in. Sybil recognized Ed Simonsen the veteran CIA agent from her adventures during the Marburg virus epidemic, especially their work together at the Washington Mall, in Canada, and during the fight leading up to the ring-leader's capture in a small town named Rutshuru in the North-Kivu province of the Democratic Republic of the Congo.

Chapter Four

"Mr. President, these are the agents from the CIA," Mrs. Novak announced.

"Have a seat, Agent Simonsen and Director Dillon. First, let me introduce Dr. Sybil Norcroft. I presume her face is as familiar at your houses as it is at mine. Agent, I understand that you and Dr. Norcroft have worked together."

The CIA officers shook Sybil's hand, and she and Ed shared a warm smile.

"I believe Dr. Norcroft is agreeable to enter into a formal—but secret, of course—agreement with the Central Intelligence Agency. I am in hopes that we can get the formalities over with in my office this morning."

Sybil nodded.

Ed signaled with a head nod that he was in favor, then deferred to his superior Andrew Dillon.

The DDCIA got right down to cases, "Dr. Norcroft, we are fully aware of the vetting process done by the FBI, including the polygraph you went through; and we presume that nothing has changed in the few months following that set of interviews. Anything to add? Any bank robberies or spying for the Bangladeshis?"

"No Sir. I'm not sure I ever met a person from Bangladesh."

"Then, I see no particular reason to repeat anything. I am obliged to tell you that this meeting with the president has not come as a surprise, and we did not come unprepared. The FBI has done an extremely thorough job of sifting through everything you have ever done, talking with every significant person with whom you have had contact, all of your writings and speeches, and have conducted a surreptitious search of your homes and offices. You have been cleared in all of the crucial areas that the Company deems to be of importance."

"Good. I can't imagine any area of my life which would disqualify me."

"We agree. As of now, you have official ultra-top secret clearance. You need to know that you must never divulge even the fact that you work for the CIA, let alone anything related to what you do now or will ever do for the Company. It will be necessary for you to sign the Official Secrets Act Agreement before we go on. You should take note of the severe penalties for failure to keep secrets or to have complete loyalty to the United States government and the Constitution."

Sybil examined the complex informational document as rapidly as she could so as not to prolong the awkward silence between her and the officers. The agreement spelled out the nature of her commitment: All information that came to her was to be considered classified and was to be conveyed only to proper authorities with a compartmentalized need to know. She was to avoid seeking additional information outside her personal professional need to know. While employed by the CIA, she was never to publish in any form any information related to the agency, its work, or the activities in which she was engaged or of which she had knowledge. After termination of her association with the Central Intelligence Agency—as spelled out in the contract—the contract agent could not publish any information even in the form of fictional writing without prior permission and censorship by the agency. The contract spelled out that the agreement was entered into during the time of war—The War on Terror—and violation of the terms—which were to be regarded as laws—could constitute acts of treason, and would be dealt with in the private agency judicial division. The stated penalties included long imprisonment and even capital punishment.

Sybil signed and initialed more than a dozen places on the documents indicating that she had read the documents and understood what was said.

The DDCIA became deadly serious, looked Sybil directly in the eyes and said, "Trust and loyalty are everything with us. This is not the Boy Scouts. We don't go in for reverence, courtesy, friendliness, cheerfulness, or even cleanliness much. But we are big on trust and loyalty—very big. You don't have to be too educated or even overly smart. Common morality may well be a drawback. The loyalty oath you just signed is a life and death thing. We have zero tolerance for traitors. There are no second chances. I know Company people that are queers, drug addicts, pedophiles, wife beaters, polygamists, card cheats, and murderers; but I don't know a single living traitor to the ranks of the Company."

He paused to let Sybil digest the import of his sermon.

The implicit and explicit threats were not lost on the neurosurgeon. She let her calm and forthright expression be her answer. She was learning.

The DDCIA continued, "Not everyone is suited for our line of work. You will be worked and tested. If you fail, you will be back in the civilian ranks, and you will forget that this experience ever happened. The quickest—the most unforgiving—way to find yourself out of the program is to fail your periodical polygraph vettings. After you are actively engaged in Company work, failing the lie detector may mean a Company trial and swift and sure justice—the least noxious result being dismissal. Any questions about the seriousness of that kind of justice?"

"None."

Sybil felt a little chilly.

"I will elaborate anyway. In the federal courts, the punishment for divulging CIA information is ten years in prison and/or a $10,000 fine. I am here to warn you that very few cases come to federal trial. We act as our own protectors; and we are our own judges, juries, and...executioners. You are going to hear the phrase 'The CIA neither confirms nor denies' used in the press frequently. That represents a lot of activity we handle ourselves. Don't worry about John Law; worry about me!"

Sybil nodded her understanding, never taking her eyes away from those hard eyes of the DDCIA and won the no-blink contest.

"Now, Dr. Norcroft, please sign this contract which contains much the same language."

Sybil barely glanced at the contract documents.

"I do not want to be a contract officer. I want to be a full-fledged regular officer of the Central Intelligence Agency with all of the obligations, responsibilities, and privileges. I have friends who have been involved with the agency and being a contract officer did not work out well. Specifically, my father served as a JAG officer during the Viet Nam war and was assigned to defend the case of contract officers who were assassins for the Phoenix Program. I am sure you are familiar with it. In brief, the Phoenix cadres were betrayed and abandoned, and the suit involved the minor case of getting their families out of the country after the collapse of the war effort in April, 1975. In the end, the CIA and the U.S. government denied their existence. There was no proof that the men were ever in the employ of the CIA or that they were ever in Viet Nam. They were erased, including their pay records which were maintained through the Department of Agriculture. Their families were left to the tender mercies of the invading NVA [North Vietnamese Army]. I want to avoid any such fate by the decisions that are made up front here today."

Her face was placid—more calm than she felt inside. She met the eyes of the president, the CIA agent, and the DDCIA. The latter was taken aback. He was angry at first, then bemused because he had presumed that the doctor was an innocent in matters pertaining to CIA policy. After a minute or so of thought, he decided that he rather admired the chutzpah of the formidable woman. He liked it, and he was beginning to like her.

He tested, "I'm afraid that you will not be able to serve in the intelligence services then, Doctor."

He folded the documents back into the manila folder and looked to the president. Sybil called his bluff in this high-stakes poker game.

She stood and said quietly and unemotionally, "Thank you, Mr. President, Gentlemen, I appreciate your time. Should you change your minds, let me know. I will not ever make reference to this meeting."

Before she could complete her turn and walk towards the Oval Office door, DDCIA Dillon stopped her.

"Perhaps we can work something out. I don't have the authority to make you a CIA officer per se. Would you sign a contract and trust me to proceed with all due diligence to see if you can qualify as a regular agent. I will take it up with my superiors, the DCIA and the NSA [National Security Advisor]."

"I do not mean any disrespect Director Dillon, but I don't trust you. I come from the west where we have a motto: Trust everyone but brand your cattle."

The president laughed out loud. Unseen by any of the others in the Oval Office he pushed a button on the desk console. The door opened, and Erin Novak leaned her head in.

"Please get NSA Broadhead."

The door closed. There was an awkward silence.

"Please take your seat again, Dr. Norcroft. I think we can iron all of this out in a matter of minutes."

Five minutes later, Mrs. Novak knocked softly, opened the door, and ushered Lt. CDR Owen Broadhead into the room.

"Owen, I believe you know the gentlemen from the CIA. Let me formally introduce you to Dr. Sybil Norcroft. You no doubt know her at least by reputation."

"Certainly, Mr. President. It is a pleasure to meet you, Dr. Norcroft."

"Commander."

They shook hands.

"Now, Commander, I have an order for you. Make Dr. Norcroft a regular officer in the Central Intelligence Agency."

"But, Mr. President," Dillon objected, "I have to have the permission of my boss, the DCIA."

"I suppose I don't have to remind you that I am your boss's boss."

"No, Sir."

"Make it happen, Commander Broadhead."

"I'll be back in a jiffy, Mr. President. I'll get the papers from my office."

The two CIA officers recognized that it was the better part of valor for them to keep quiet.

Lt. CDR Broadhead returned promptly with the new set of papers. Even the paper was more important; this time, the document was on parchment, and already contained the signature of Martin Edelweiss, the DCIA. He handed the papers to the president.

President Willets handed them to DDCIA Dillon, "Please have the prospective agent sign the papers, Director Dillon."

Dillon gracefully submitted the documents to Sybil who signed them with alacrity. The president sat back down at the Resolute desk—a large, nineteenth-century partners' desk which President Willets and many of his predecessors used during their terms of office. It was a clear signal that the meeting was over.

Outside the Oval Office in the West Wing hallway, DDCIA Dillon looked at Sybil with respect and said, "Welcome to the CIA, Agent Norcroft. You are hereby assigned to the Counterintelligence Threat Analysis Division. Your title will be Field Officer. You showed real moxie and resourcefulness today, Agent. We have been wondering whether or not you have it in you to do the first mission we want you to do. Today's performance has convinced me. Please come to my office at Langley at ten sharp on Monday. That's it for today."

Ed Simonsen walked slowly enough to let the DDCIA leave the White House first.

He caught up to Sybil and said quietly, "You won today. Only time will tell if you have created a friend or an enemy in Director Dillon. He is good at both ends of that spectrum. Congratulations on your appointment."

Chapter Five

S ybil Norcroft, M.D., Ph.D., F.A.C.S. received a disturbing formal letter from the American Association of Neurological Surgeons [AANS]. The letter was short and to the point: Sybil's activities working for Wolf News, helping to eradicate the Marburg virus epidemic, helping the CDC find and capture the ring leader of the al Qaeda cell who perpetrated the biological terrorism plot, and her two year long fight to defend herself against the spurious charges of murder for which she was jailed, indicted, tried, and finally acquitted, had resulted in her having done only three neurosurgical operations in four years.

The letter concluded with a warning and an exhortation: "Dr. Norcroft, although we fully acknowledge your past and current services to the AANS and the high esteem in which you are held by your colleagues around the world, we must remind you of a pertinent and important rule set out in the policies of the association. To maintain your membership in the AANS, and to retain hospital privileges recognized by the association, you must perform a minimum of eleven neurosurgical procedures each calendar year. Of those operations, four must be craniotomies. Your alternative would be to leave the active practice of neurosurgery and to assume a retirement status in the AANS, which would no longer require you to pay annual dues. In order to continue active practice, you must perform the requisite number of surgeries for the next four years, obtain 30 hours of CME [Continuing Medical Education] credit annually during that period and thereafter. In short, you are hereby informed that your status in the AANS is probationary. If you elect to continue your career in the operating room, your performance in every case for the next two years must be monitored by a designated AANS monitor, and that progress reported to the Executive Committee of the association during that time.

"Please find attached a list of AANS monitors in your state. You must make arrangements to begin the monitoring process in no more than thirty days and begin your monitored surgical schedule in no less than sixty days from the date of this notice."

There were only four names on the enclosed list. She had to shudder when she saw that one of them was Raza Patel, her foremost competitor among neurosurgeons, media medical consultants, and for the limelight. Although Dr. Patel's main professional practice privileges were at the Weill Cornell Medical School Hospitals in New York City—an institution closed to Sybil—he also had privileges at Columbia University and operated there occasionally when a patient's insurance required that the surgery only be done at Columbia. When Sybil received the Alfred I. duPont-Columbia University Award honoring excellence in broadcast and digital journalism, she had taken the regents up on their offer to have limited privileges in the operating room. That was the only place she had privileges; and, of the names on the AANS list, only Raza Patel also had privileges there.

Sybil would rather have eaten a plate of overcooked crow—feathers and all—than to have to admit her conundrum to her competitor. It would be a major loss of face to have to do so, and would put her in a position of owing a huge favor to a potential nemesis, if he, indeed, even agreed to help her. In this one aspect of her life, Raza Patel held her future, and could probably exact a serious favor in return—like cutting back on her successful work at Wolf News to allow him to regain his edge in the ratings. Sybil was not ready to give up surgery. It had poured too much of herself into getting to where she was in the profession to throw it all away now… yet. She gritted her teeth and did what she had to do.

Although television stations closely guard communications with their stars, Sybil's name and fame greased the skids; and she was able to get Dr. Patel's cell phone number with relative ease. That was one hurdle passed that decreased her rising stress level.

"Raza Patel speaking," the voice familiar to every educated person on the planet said after two rings.

"Dr. Patel, this is Sybil Norcroft from Wolf News. I would appreciate a moment of your time to discuss a personal problem of mine."

"Neurosurgical?"

"Only indirectly, Dr. Patel…"

"Please call me Raza, all my friends do," he said.

His response was so genuine and friendly that Sybil was afraid her voice would crack.

"And I'm Sybil. Thank you for that. My problem is that my success in the media world has put me into trouble with the AANS. I haven't done enough surgery over the past four years to keep up my active membership, and now maybe even my medical license could be in jeopardy. I need your help."

"You have it, Sybil, what can I do?"

His response was so open, uncondescending, and solicitous that Sybil's emotions began to come through in her voice.

"I can't tell you…how much that means to me, Raza. I have always greatly admired you for what you have accomplished; and when I became a modest competitor, I was afraid that you would not appreciate my arrival on the media scene. I misjudged you for no good reason."

"And, apparently, I have done the same thing, Sybil. You know about my stupid private comment—that became all too public—about you being a solipsist."

Sybil just laughed, "I had to look it up in *Websters New World Unabridged Dictionary*—my iPhone dictionary wasn't that smart."

"Well, at least I got a little one-up-mans-ship on you with that. But, seriously, how can I help you."

"Maybe the phone is not the best way for us to discuss my problem. How about I take you to lunch at some dive where the paparazzi can't find us?"

"I know just the place—good food, no ambience, and no self-respecting paparazzo would allow himself to be found dead in the joint. How about today?"

"That would be wonderful, Raza. You're a prince."

"Not everyone pronounces it that way, but thanks for the thought. I'll pick you up at the Wolf News studios at noon, okay?"

"Great."

The restaurant—Dinos and Daves Grill in Spanish Harlem—was perfect. It was actually clean and present-able, and the food was surprisingly good. Sybil and Raza finished their meal before getting down to business. It took Sybil ten minutes to explain her predicament and the two of them another fifteen minutes to work out the details of their collaboration. Sybil's estimation of Raza Patel, the media star, had increased in stratospheric proportions by the time their lunch date was over. He could not have been more a gentleman and a genuinely accommodating colleague. He even got on his cell to let three of his patients who had been waiting a year to have surgery know that he had a great alternative for them. Less than an hour after entering Dinos and Daves, Sybil's problem with the AANS was on its way to being solved.

"I can't tell you how much I appreciate what you are doing for me, Raza. I think I can return the favor in a mutually beneficial way. Wolf News and I are in the planning stages of a medical news series about head injuries. We plan to be quite controversial in the first program and report the developing trend to do away with high school football. There is considerable information out there. It's going to be provocative; but if the two of us become the faces of the movement to protect our children, it might just grow legs. What do you think?"

"I have to laugh about that. WWN has been toying with the same idea for two years. The execs have been too chicken to go ahead because of the huge popularity of the sport. I am personally of the opinion that too many kids are being maimed mentally or getting their necks broken, and the U.S. should make some serious societal changes. I know that some Texas schools—of all places—have done away with football just because it costs so much and is interfering with the schools' ability to provide a complete education to the youth in their communities. If we were to join forces, it could possibly become part of the national debate. Let's do it, my friend, if that is not too presumptive of me to call you that," Raza said.

"It's an honor, Raza. I see great things coming out of our collaborations—plural. Let's go back to our offices and start to beat up on the execs."

They clinked their glasses of Perrier as a token of sealing a deal.

Ed Simonsen was in DDCIA Dillon's office in the CIA headquarters in Langley on Monday morning when Sybil arrived. The two men stood for her when Dillon's office assistant showed her in.

"Thanks for being on time. It's a busy day; so, I don't want to waste much time on chit-chat," Dillon said.

Ed and Sybil nodded.

"Ed is going to take you to the secret Company training facility—The Farm—next Monday morning. You will need to be there for three weeks of condensed training. Sometime in the future you will need to take the entire three month course to become fully certified as a field officer; but right now, we have a project for you; and we will have to concentrate on getting you ready for that. Think you can get away from the cameras for that long without having to explain what you are up to?"

"I'll lie and tell them I have to take a vacation. In fact, I have one coming, and I will take an extra week to go camping with my husband and little girl."

"That's the spirit. Our motto here is, 'If you can't accomplish your communication without lying, just keep mum.' You're going to fit right in, it appears. And just take a small bag with outdoors clothes, the medicines you need, an extra pair of glasses, and a watch. You won't be needing a lap-top, an iPad, or a cell phone. There will be a couple of advantages of this "vacation" on the Company's dime: you will lose weight and get a tan, and you won't have time to worry about your profession or your family. It'll be great!"

Ed laughed, then Andrew Dillon laughed with him. It was a conspiratorial laugh.

Chapter Six

Charles scouted around in the campsite for dead-fall wood to keep the campfire going strongly while Sybil taught Cerisse how to make s'mores. The chocolate, marshmellow, and graham cracker guilty delights were the best sweets Cerisse had ever tasted. The very word meant excess—s'more chocolate, s'more marshmellow, and s'more graham crackers. Until she was fourteen and was adopted by Sybil and Charles and brought to the United States from the Congo, she had hardly ever tasted a sweet aside from a few sucks on a used sugar cane. In fact, before coming to the U.S., the diminutive pygmy girl had scarcely had a pleasant day. While working to thwart the al Qaeda-Fabrique Pharmaceutique DRC plot to cause a Marburg virus spread misère, Sybil had also saved tiny, fetching Cerisse from her life of enslavement and sexual bondage. The love between the two of them was boundless. Cerisse had an understandable fear and dislike of men, but Charles had won her over in a couple of months. Now, he was "Daddy", and she was usually, "Sweetheart". She looked to the agri-business mogul as her towering protector.

The smell of the pine and maple smoke mixed with the rich odors of the earth and trees was tranquilizing for all three of them. It was their first family vacation in three years, and vacation was an altogether new concept to the previously deprived child for whom the kindness of a stranger who might have given her a discarded toy was more than she had experienced. The three days of backpacking in the Three Top Mountain Loop area northwest of Washington D.C. would—for the rest of Cerisse's life—count high among the experiences she treasured as being days of pure and unspoiled happiness.

"Let me tell you something I memorized the first time I ever went camping," Sybil said to Cerisse. "It is from a book called *On Walden Pond*, by a man named Henry David Thoreau. 'I went to the woods because I wished to live life deliberately. I wanted to live deep and suck out all the marrow of life. To put to rout all that was not life. And not, when I came to die, discover that I had not lived.'"

"I understand, Mama. I feel the same way about the three of us being here. I know you and Daddy are very busy, and it is so wonderful for us to be alone and away from everybody else. I am not afraid. I trust you and Daddy. I have enough to eat—enough for three of my girl-friends. I don't have to hide food for fear that there won't be enough for tomorrow. And the men can't come here."

She shed a few salty tears of joy, and Sybil did the same. They walked until they were exhausted each day having sucked the marrow of life out of a three-day week full of such days. The last half of the last day, Cerisse was so worn out that Charles put her on his shoulders and carried her the last five miles back to the car. She was stiff and sore all over when she returned to Georgetown Visitation Preparatory School the day after the Daniels family got back to the real world.

She even loved the ache of her muscles because the ache was a reminder of the best days of her life thus far.

Sybil performed three craniotomies—fortunately relatively simple removals of superficial tumors—with her new friend Raza Patel tactfully monitoring her. In truth, Sybil realized she had gotten a bit rusty, and confessed that truth to Raza. He was taken with her humility, and their friendship blossomed. He sent glowing reports to the monitoring committee of the AANS, and it was clear that Sybil's clinical professional life was getting back on track.

On Monday, at three a.m., Ed picked her up in his Subaru; and they drove to Andrews Air Force base where they boarded a Navy Seahawk SH-60 helicopter and were flown to the small landing strip at Camp Peary—The Farm. Camp Peary as it is named officially—but better known as The Farm by insiders—is located northeast of the city of Williamsburg, Virginia on the west bank of the York River off Route 5, close to Allmondsville and Croaker. It is an official secret of the CIA, but to no one else apparently. It is enclosed in a twenty-five square mile section of wilderness Virginia running between the highway and the river. The facility serves as a huge training site for CIA agents, infiltrators, covert operators, and for special ops military units as diverse as SEALS, Army Rangers, and Special Forces, Viet Nam war PRU leader trainees, and the Delta Force. Its location is openly discussed by locals and regularly pointed out to tourists. About the only persons unfamiliar with its location are those totally devoid of curiosity, newly arrived, nonpolitical, nonmilitary immigrants, and ardent right-wing religious zealots who accept the fiction of a benign U.S. foreign policy.

The helicopter was met by men in olive drab uniforms lacking rank or service insignia. Ed and Sybil climbed aboard a Humvee and were driven to an isolated area of the camp property. No one spoke a word. The two men indicated to the two passengers that they should get out of the vehicle, and pointed at the small government building fifty yards away.

Once inside, Sybil was fingerprinted, weighed and measured, photographed front and profile, had a DNA sample swabbed from the mucosa inside her cheek, and put through a very efficient and thorough physical and laboratory examination by four doctors and four nurses. She was inoculated for small-pox, cholera, yellow fever, and three unpronounceable tropical illnesses. She had x-rays taken of her chest, skull, spine, and a complete set of dental pictures. Both shoulders ached from the injections. As she sat through the boring examination, she became aware of a poster on the white wall of the clinic. It read:

> What you see here,
> What you hear here,
> What you do here,
> Stays here,
> When you leave here.

"Welcome to Camp Peary, Dr. Norcroft. Nice to see you again, John," a patrician grey-haired man said.

He was looking at Ed when he said the name 'John', and Sybil was pretty sure that he had not made a mistake.

That opinion was verified when the man said, "My name is John Smith."

It occurred to Sybil that when the people training in Camp Peary lined up in alphabetical order, the "S" line would have been inordinately long.

"You are assigned to room 1CT, which is in the next building to the south. Please stow your gear there and come back here. We need to get started; so, move right along."

When she stepped back outside, she noted that every person she saw was running; so, she covered the fifty yards to her room and back at a brisk pace. She found a pair of camouflage BDUs and boots that fit; and, taking the hint, she changed into them. In the battle dress uniform, she felt like she belonged and adopted something like the same swagger she saw in the gait of the people running around her.

"You are here for the much abbreviated Farm course. We will start each day of your three week stay with a run and a brisk workout, a hearty breakfast, and then we will get down to work. Please take notes, but know that the notes have to stay here when you leave here. Do not attempt to take photographs. If you have an electronic gadget, including a cellular telephone, surrender it now. If you have one tomorrow, you will be escorted from the facility and may face charges. Any questions?"

Sybil shook her head side-to-side signifying, "no".

"Our electronics experts are here now; so, that's where we'll get started. What you need to know about the electronic devices you will use on your mission will be extremely simple. In fact, it is better that you know little. That way you cannot divulge anything useful under duress."

The reality of her involvement with the spy agency was beginning to sink in. She did not like to think about being 'under duress'.

The young Chinese woman who was to serve as her instructor did not even attempt to teach Sybil how the specialized thumb drive she was going to receive worked more than just to know what to do with it.

"The USB flash drive is a data storage device that includes flash memory with an integrated [Universal Serial Bus] interface. Like ordinary USB flash drives this one is rewritable, and physically much smaller than an optical disc. Yours looks every bit like a lipstick tube, and the point of it includes real pink lipstick. The lipstick can be removed easily to reveal the retractable metal connector. There is enough room below the actual lipstick to allow you to grip the device for its purpose without getting the lipstick dye on your fingers."

Ed served only as an observer. The Chinese woman—who was not named John Smith, but might as well have been—was called Wang Fang [aromatous] as were more than 270 thousand other Chinese females. It was the equivalent of the American "Jane Doe". Presumably the "D" line would be overcrowded in the Asian section when lines formed alphabetically at the Farm. She and Sybil worked almost a hundred times on the smoothest and least obtrusive way to insert the USB into an advanced Russian [Soviet] MIR series of desktop computers. Sybil could have gone through the motions with her eyes closed, maybe even in her sleep, by the time Wang Fang pronounced Sybil proficient.

"I know this is deadly boring, but you will only have one quick chance to insert the flash drive into the computer's USB port. Remember to leave it in place for almost five minutes to collect all of the data from the computer's hard drive. You will have to choose your timing very carefully. Your USB has 512 GB [gigabytes of memory]—plenty for the task—but it will be taking in so much data, that it will take a few minutes."

Wang Fang—or whoever she was—reached into a drawer and pulled out a piece of black silk cloth and showed Sybil a small pocket hidden in a pleated fold. The pocket had a fine toothed plastic zipper. When the USB drive was inserted into the pocket and the pocket zipped up, it was almost invisible. Sybil was ordered to place the USB drive into the pocket over and over again until she could do it without looking at or fumbling for the pocket of her evening gown or its zipper.

"You will have a very nice black silk evening gown which shows some diverting cleavage—which you will have to provide—and a pocket exactly like this one in the cloth over your left hip. With the diversion you provide in your dress, you should be able to keep the men's eyes on the diversion and the women's looking green-eyed with jealousy into your eyes to ascertain what your intentions are towards their men. If you are not able to be completely alone when you insert the USB into the computer port, that diversion may prove to be indispensable. Tomorrow you get fitted into the dress. Our seamstresses and tailors here are among the best in the world."

"What is the purpose of putting the USB flash drive into the Russian computer?"

"Good question, and I will answer simply. It is a very special device—nifty little thing—which will suck the computer dry of its information without leaving a trace of having been there. For all intents and purposes, no one will be able tell that the computer has been hacked. And…they will not recognize that a virus has been installed. This is a totally nondestructive virus that allows our cyberwarfare people to monitor Russian electronic information traffic without the Russians ever being the wiser. It is not a weapon in the sense that the old Stuxnet virus was. You probably remember that Stuxnet was very successful and posed a severe risk; it boomeranged. We won't get hoist by our own petard this go-around."

"What if I get caught?"

"Don't. You are going to have a bit of dental work just in case, however. If it is clear that you have been exposed, you will bite down on your second molar on the right, and all your last memory will be the taste and smell of bitter almonds."

"Cyanide," Sybil said.

"Indeed…such an ugly word."

During the second week, Sybil went through a crash course in the use of poisons. She learned that she was being given that sophisticated information for a later mission.

The wizened professorial instructor limited his lecture and practical demonstrations to naturally occurring cone snail toxins.

"All of the some 500 cone sea snails, family *Conidae*, are poisonous. The creatures of concern are the large ones—especially those whose various conotoxins are lethal—including a venom that contains a pain-reducing toxin which the snail uses to pacify the victim before immobilizing and then killing it. Some cone snail venoms—the ones we have an interest in—contain tetradoxin—TTX, for short—the paralytic sodium channel blocker neurotoxin found in pufferfish, the blue-ringed octopus, and the Oregon rough-skinned newt, which are about as deadly a set of creatures as ever evolved. We have taken a few liberties with the components of the toxins and *voila!*, we have produced a toxin that—unlike the entirely naturally occurring peptide—when it is rubbed on the skin or ingested in amounts comparable to a droplet the size of a pencil eraser results in death before the victim takes two steps…You no doubt know of the vicious little Vietnamese green tree snake?"

"I've heard of it," said Sylvia, "isn't that the two-step snake?"

"That is, in fact, a myth; but this toxin is quite literally the real thing. You have a vial of it mixed with the improved cone

snail TTX. Don't make a mistake and get some on yourself—
no fingers in the mouth or rubbing your eyes; those are fatal
errors. In addition to oral or transdermal installation, the
newly improved conotoxin can be injected, just as the nasty
marine gastropod mollusks do with their ghastly tooth that
they use like a harpoon. Makes one shudder. Since the worst
creatures are endemic to California, we are able to harvest a
truly impressive number of poison sacs; so, you can be down-
right wasteful; but I remind you again, you can only be care-
less once. You will be in a place we know as the "Kingdom
of Hatred" when you make use of it. Like the Russians, the
people you will meet there are very unforgiving. I cannot
tell you more right now, but your shadow, John—Sybil read
Ed—will brief you when you need to know."

Chapter Seven

Sybil and the U.S. Surgeon General, Milton Armstrong, were scheduled to be co-keynote speakers at the International Forum on Global Health Issues in Moscow a month from the time she finished her training at The Farm. Sybil was slated to speak to the general assembly on trauma as a healthcare issue, particularly in children, and Gen. Armstrong's title was "Has Sport Become a Risk to Global Health and Economies". During the month that led up to their departure for Moscow, Gen. Armstrong barnstormed around the country to promote the discontinuation of high school football in favor of less serious trauma producing sports. He traded on his built-in admiration and name-recognition inherited from such illustrious predecessors in his offices as C. Everett Koop in the nineteen-eighties, who made it his life's goal to educate Americans about the dangers and costs of tobacco use, and Regina Benjamin, who served her four year term from 2009 to 2013. She focused her attention and that of her fellow-Americans on prevention. Under Dr. Benjamin's leadership, implementation of the *National Prevention Strategy* in 2011 became a practical reality. Using her education and experience as a rural family practitioner, her initiative provided an unprecedented opportunity to shift the nation from a focus on sickness and disease to one based on wellness and prevention. Her vision paper, *The Surgeon General's Vision for a Healthy and Fit Nation* (2010), showed Americans how to choose nutritious food, add more physical activity to their daily lives, and an assortment of ways to manage stress. Gen. Armstrong—the fourth African-American to be appointed to the office of Surgeon General—was tireless in his pursuit of education for the American public in matters related to trauma and how young people and the elderly can protect themselves from one of the major causes of death and disability. He spent his month stumping the country to spread his message.

Sybil used her bully-pulpit at Wolf News to warn people about the dangers of traumatic injury and how to prevent major injuries. In agreement with Gen. Armstrong, she began a slow but determined push to get football out of the nation's high schools. Her major coup was to enlist the support of Raza Patel on WWN. He agreed with Sybil and Gen. Armstrong, and the three prominent figures became a unified powerful voice of caution about trauma. The global health care community took serious note of what the three of them were doing and what they were talking about. The Secretary General of the United Nations and the Director-General of the World Health Organization agreed to underwrite the costs and advertising for the upcoming meetings in Moscow and asked both Sybil and Gen. Armstrong if they would have any objections to Dr. Raza Patel sharing center stage with them in several meetings during the forum. The two leaders were candid about the value to the project that would come from having all three famous and photogenic Americans appearing in a united front. Their presence would guarantee a strong media coverage for what was going to be billed as a star-studded world event.

Ed Simonsen and the DDCIA were ecstatic at the high profile billing for their agent, and enthusiastically endorsed the plans for the three prominent American physicians to meet the world, and more importantly to them, to mingle freely around the Kremlin. They reasoned that Sybil should have no difficulty in finding an opportunity to meet alone with the secure computers in the offices of the SVR [Foreign Intelligence Service, Russia's primary external intelligence agency—the successor of the First Chief Directorate—PGU—of the Soviet KGB].

The SVR is responsible for intelligence and espionage activities outside the Russian Federation. It works in cooperation with the GRU [Main Intelligence Directorate] which deploys spies in foreign countries. The SVR is also authorized to negotiate anti-terrorist cooperation and intelligence-sharing arrangements with foreign intelligence agencies, and provides analysis and dissemination of intelligence to the Russian president, Afonasii Glebovich Tikhondnko.

Sybil was scheduled to hold an exclusive seminar on the problems of alcohol abuse in the Kremlin building that housed the FSB [Russian Federal Security Service] whose main responsibilities are within the country and include counter-intelligence, internal and border security, counter-terrorism, and surveillance as well as investigating some types of grave crimes. Taken together, access to their interlinked computer system would be an espionage feat rivaling anything ever accomplished by the U.S. intelligence services; and Sybil was in a perfect position to pull it off.

Sybil made a concerted effort to spend as much time as possible with Charles and Cerisse to assuage their concerns and their objections to her being away from them. Charles told her that he had not counted on such a heavy travel schedule when he agreed to give his blessing to her employment at Wolf News. He knew nothing about her involvement with the CIA.

Cerisse was mollified when Sybil told her, "I will only be gone for six days. You can watch everything I do on the news, and we can Skype every day. You are busy in school, and the time will pass by quickly."

"I suppose so," the energetic girl agreed reluctantly but had a facial expression that suggested that there was more on her mind.

"I know you too well, Cerisse, what's up?"

"Oh, nothing. Well, maybe a little something."

"Like what?"

"Well, I was thinking how neat it would be if you came by and spoke at an assembly at my school before you go. You could talk about going to Russia to help them and about your Marburg virus adventures and all of that stuff. What do you think?"

"Who am I to resist you, my devious little daughter? Sure. Make arrangements for Thursday morning. I leave on Saturday morning, and I haven't had a minute to pack."

"I already did," Cerisse said with an impish grin.

Sybil laughed and determined to give Cerisse's classmates at the exclusive girl's school an exciting insight into the world that awaits such intelligent and industrious young women.

The nonstop Delta flight from New York's John F. Kennedy International Airport to Sheremetyevo International Airport in Moscow was a comfortable first-class experience for Sybil and Raza, who sat next to each other and became fully acquainted during the flight. Sybil did not see Ed or anyone else that resembled her mental concept of a CIA operative. That was relaxing, but she did have a concern in the back of her mind that she did not yet have the USB flash drives she needed to do her spy work. She figured that Ed would come through when it was safe and unobtrusive.

He did. After they passed through passport and visa control, Sybil, Raza, and Milton—by then they were all on a first name basis—hired two porters to take them to one of the pick-up kiosks in front of the massive airport. A large black convertible stretch limousine pulled up in front of the kiosk. The large vehicle was new—a remake of the pride of the Soviet Union Zil—and was flying the colors of the United Nations and the World Health Organization. Their arrival had obviously been leaked to the paparazzi who descended on them. The driver—in full Russian professional driver livery—got out of the car and issued commands that dispersed the crowd of journalists. His copper identification tag bore the name of Edvard Tisgler, but the man's face was that of Edgar Simonsen. He bade them welcome both in English and in unaccented Russian. Sybil restrained herself from flashing a knowing smile.

The keynote addresses took place that evening in the conference halls of The Grand Kremlin Palace. Its five reception halls—Georgievsky, Vladimirsky, Aleksandrovsky, Andreyevsky, and Ekaterininsky—were fully opened to accommodate the huge crowd of global health care officials, Russian dignitaries, and paparazzi from news services around the world. There was heavy security everywhere. Sybil and Raza followed obediently behind the Surgeon General—whose Lieutenant

General's uniform was the equal in rank to any other military officer in the building. He was accorded due deference, and the members of the reception line presumed that Sybil and Raza were there largely at his behest. When Sylvia paused to shake the hand of Colonel General Yevgeni Mitrokhin, the Director of the SVR, she felt a slight tug on her skirt on the left side. She glanced very quickly in the direction of the tug. Because she was so close to such a high ranking general, his security guards pressed in more closely. On her left was a stern-faced guard looking straight ahead. His name tag read "Dobronravov", but his face read "Simonsen". She was amazed at the ingenuity of her CIA mentor, partner, and friend and the resources the Company provided. She maintained an expression on her face as bland as a rice cracker.

"Greetings and welcome to the *Rossiyskaya Federatsiya*, Dr. Norcroft. Your reputation has preceded you. I look forward to hearing your talk. We here in the Russian Federation have heard fine things about your abilities to inform, educate, and entertain your audiences," Gen. Mitokhin said and smiled.

"It is entirely my pleasure, General. The highly vaunted Russian hospitality has been in full force. Thank you."

The tug at her skirt ceased. She ventured a quick feel of where she knew the nearly invisible zippered pocket lay tucked into an adroitly situated pleat. She could make out the form of three thumb drives. She was unsure whether to be relieved or worried; but at least *alea iacta est* [the die is cast] for good or for evil.

Gen. Mitrokhin turned toward the President of the Russian Federation, "Mr. President, I have the honor to present the remarkable Sybil Norcroft, M.D., Ph.D., F.A.C.S., currently the chief medical consultant for the American Wolf News Network."

President Afonasii Glebovich Tikhondnko, a famous war hero from the Afghanistan campaign, was a dour and formidable mustachioed man who struck fear into his enemies and grudging respect in his subjects. He was overtly affable to Sybil, however.

"Greetings and *dobro pozhalovat'* [welcome], my dear," he said. "We are looking forward to your presentations. Afterwards, I would like to invite you to a small reception in the Royal Apartments."

"I would be honored," she said.

With that, the press of attendees behind her moved her forward.

Drs. Armstrong, Patel, and Norcroft were the only speakers in the United Nations/W.H.O. forum that evening. When they finished, the assembled attendees, including the Russian dignitaries, gave them a long and enthusiastic standing ovation. That was unusual to the point of being almost unheard of for a scientific presentation in Moscow. The three Americans were photographed and interviewed by dozens of print and electronic media journalists; and before they dropped exhausted into their beds, the entire world was able to see them and to rehash the concepts they espoused. Sybil and Raza's ratings soared—Sybil's just slightly more than her new friend and WWN competitor's.

President Tikhondnko's security guard escorted Sybil to the Royal Apartments in the Terem Palace. The other Americans were not invited. Sybil was sure that this was her moment and was uneasy because Ed was nowhere around; she was entirely on her own. She was sweating lightly; but upon inspection, she was pleased to see that her hands were not trembling.

The first dignitary who spoke to her was an odd fellow who was dressed in a tuxedo, but introduced himself as General Ioannu Konstantinevsky Unkovsky. It took only a few minutes for Sybil to understand that the man was the equivalent of the American Surgeon General.

"I have held various positions in health inspection before becoming—a few years ago—the deputy health minister and chief sanitary doctor of the Russian Republic, I am proud to tell you that I have been a passionate promoter of food patriotism in Russia. Mine has been the voice of warning for my country's citizens against indulging in alternative foreign cuisines such as sushi, quiche, and McDonald's fast food. I also regularly have campaigned against alcohol use. I am a staunch advocate of natural foods but earlier this year I had to exhort my Russian countrymen not to eat snow."

He was drinking a steaming cup of tea.

"That looks good," Sybil said trying to make polite conversation.

"Yes," he said, "it is tea brewed from snow."

Apparently, he did not see any inconsistency between his exhortation and his own dietary preferences; so, Sybil let it go.

The president was busy with the dozens of carefully selected guests, all of whom clamored for his attention. Sybil walked about the sumptuous rooms admiring the magnificent Russian art.

"Quite remarkable," came the deep and unmistakable baritone of President Tikhondnko's commanding stentorian voice.

"They certainly are. It is wonderful that you were able to preserve some many from the Imperial Era, the time of the Bolsheviks when so much was lost, and from the chaotic period of transition during *perestroika* [restructuring] and *glasnost* [openness], and finally into the current era. Congratulations to you and the Russian people."

Sybil meant what she said, and it came across as genuine and not sycophantic as did most of what the president heard every day. It pleased him.

"I have a little something for you and your friends," the president said and beckoned to a uniformed servant.

President Tikhondnko took an ornate box from the servant and handed it to Sybil. She smiled and nodded.

"Thank you, Sir, this is most kind."

"Open the boxes, please, Doctor. I want to share in the pleasure this small token brings."

The opened box revealed a quintessentially Russian plate—three Villeroy & Boch Heinrich Russian Fairy Tales Plates depicting the Snegurochka Snow Maiden. It was exquisite.

"I don't know what to say, Mr. President. It is beautiful. It will be a treasured heirloom in our family for generations to come."

She had obviously said the right thing. President Tikhondnko beamed and gave her a small bow.

"It is a real pleasure to talk with you, Doctor. Unfortunately, I have to 'press the flesh' as your politicians like to say. Enjoy the Royal Apartments. Wander about and take in as much of it as you can. Perhaps one day we can meet again in your country. I would love to have you show me around the Grand Canyon and especially Las Vegas—the sin city."

They both laughed.

"Do you know those places?"

"I do. And it would be fun to amaze you in our country's national parks and to amuse you in the gambling capital of the world. I have to warn you; you will have to hold on to your money and count your fingers while you are there."

An aide came to draw the reluctant president away.

"I'll take you up on the offer, Doctor. It should be fun," President Tikhondnko said quietly in parting.

This was her moment. As soon as the president and his retinue disappeared into the heavy drinking crowd, she began to look for his office. Oddly, for such an important man and such a secure place, almost every room was wide open. Probably that was because there was art work to enthrall a connoisseur in every room—from the oil paintings to the statuary to the marvelous gilded Russian historical furniture. The openness was also an expression of trust. Only fully vetted people—mainly the president's friends—were invited; and no one would have dared or even thought of the possibility of violating the implicit security protocols.

Except the American spy, Sybil Norcroft. She trembled a little at the implications of what she was about to do.

It took her half an hour to make her way to where Ed Simonsen had described would be the very secure and very personal office of the most powerful man in Russia and the equal in power, authority, and vindictiveness of any person in the world. There was little to attract the casual visitor into the hallway leading to the office; and the further Sybil walked, the fewer people she encountered. She had expected a phalanx of tough Cossacks to be on guard at the office; but instead, there were only two bored and mildly intoxicated men standing by the door. Sybil had heeded the suggestion from Ed to carry a platter of Villeroy & Boch Champagne Flutes filled to the brim with premium Krug bubbly. She balanced the platter on her gift box.

Sybil flashed the two men a winning smile and a medium but diverting glimpse of her décolletage as she pretended to stagger a little on her pencil-thin high heels. One of the guards stepped to her side and took the platter and steadied her with his large hard hand.

"Thank you, kind sir," she said in French, hoping that they would not think of her as an American should the question of her presence ever come up. "Would you and your comrade care to have these nice flutes of champagne?"

Would they ever! They had been drinking harsh Russian vodka all evening, and even on their modest incomes, they could recognize fine quality when they saw it. The men were not shy. They took the entire platter. By the time Sybil made it to the end of the hall, all six flutes were drained. No dainty sipping for those strapping young men. By the time she walked back along the opposite wall, one of them had already achieved full bladder capacity and had to leave his fellow guard for a hasty trip to the bathroom. The other guard walked into the president's outer office and disappeared behind a row of metal filing cabinets.

Sybil heard him turn on a nice set of Russian pop song recordings. He started with *Wake Me Up!* by Avicii and was happily humming along as Sybil slipped silently on her bare feet to the row of computers in the far end of the opposite side of the office. He was singing along to the rousing sounds of *A Little Party Never Killed Nobody (All We Got)* by Fergie, Q-Tip, and Goonrock as she inserted the clandestine USB flash drive into the largest computer—the one she and Ed Simonsen had studied about and practiced on during her training at The Farm. The five minute wait was interminable, and Sybil was sweating profusely before it was time to withdraw it. *La La La* by Naughty Boy & Sam Smith was filling the air when she began her return to the outer door to the president's inner office.

The guard who had been to the bathroom first returned and announced loudly that it was the other guard's turn to go. As soon as he left, the first guard changed the song to *Young And Beautiful* by Lana Del Rey. He was sleepy and a bit befuddled by all of the alcohol he had consumed and wanted something quiet.

Sybil moved swiftly to the door and peaked out enough to be sure that neither guard was aware that she had been inside the room. She stepped out into the hall with her heart in her throat. Her luck was holding. She replaced her shoes, made sure she had a secure hold on the beautiful gift the president had given her, and began moving as swiftly away from the office as she could without attracting attention.

Behind her, from the door to the president's office, came a harsh call, "Hey, beautiful, want to party with the two of us. We can take you places those girlie Frenchy boys don't even know about!"

Sybil turned and gave the ardent drunk a saucy smile and a cautionary finger shake. He laughed—nothing ventured, nothing gained, and no harm done. She disappeared around the corner and was promptly forgotten.

Chapter Eight

The following day, Colonel General Yevgeni Mitrokhin, the Director of the SVR, sent a car to bring Sybil, Raza, and Gen. Armstrong for a tour of his headquarters building, another impressive but blocky Soviet style government edifice of the Russian Federation. The SVR [*Sluzhba Vneshney Razvedki*—Russian Foreign Intelligence Service] headquarters is located in the Yasenevo District of the far southwest corner of Moscow. Yasenevo is the most populous of Moscow's neighborhoods—and one of the most crowded—which enables the SVR to fade into the background of the bustling and prosperous section of the nation's capital city. The agents and staff of the secret service mingle comfortably with the other citizens in the neighborhood's many parks, children's playgrounds, zoos, and aquariums, and handsome restored old czarist era homes. The SVR headquarters itself is a huge and intentionally forbidding building which is enough reminiscent of the old KGB era to keep the curious well away from it.

The first thing Sybil noticed when the security guards led them into the main lobby of the building was a plaque honoring Herald "Kim" Philby—the high ranking member of MI6, the "third man" double agent—who served as both an NKVD and KGB operative, and British traitor who dealt his home country a devastating blow when he carried away the secrets of his homeland. He defected to the Soviet Union in 1963. She had a passing thought about what the man must have felt and how afraid he must have been of being exposed all those years of his treachery. She felt some of that as she entered the inner sanctum of Russia's spy apparatus. She felt very vulnerable.

Gen. Mitrokhin met Sybil, Raza, and Milton in his private office. The powerful spymaster was all bluff and blustery hale-fellow-well-met; effusive with his praise, back-slapping, and raucous jokes. He laughed and smiled constantly. However, Sybil noticed that while his mouth and the rest of his face smiled, his eyes did not. Those grey eyes took in everything and everyone without giving away anything. There was a chilly note of the sinister about him, she thought, despite all of the excessive camaraderie. Apparently, he had not completed his course at charm school.

"Velcome, velcome, my frents!" the general enthused. "I yam zo honored to be able to show you about our vacility. Ve are understandably fery broud of vhat ve haf accomplished here. It vill be a bleasure to be your guite today!"

"Thank you for making us feel welcome," Gen. Armstrong answered for the Americans.

"I hurt an amusing story about you, Dr. Norcroft. It seems that many of your colleagues refer to you as "The Snow Queen". Is that not zo?"

"I have heard that," Sybil replied with civility she did entirely feel.

"Perhaps it is not meant entirely as a compliment in your country, but here in da Rodina [Mother Russia] it is considered an affectionate description. *The Snow Queen* is a 1957 Soviet cartoon-type film directed by our famous Lev Atamanov. It was produced at da Soyuzmultfilm studio in Moscow."

"I have studied that in school," Sybil said, "it's based on the story by the Dane, Hans Christian Andersen, isn't it, General?"

"Indeed, zo, my dear. I am heppy that you are familiar with the stories that show da heart of the motherland. As you remember, it is a fairy tale which tells off da chourney a modest little Russian girl named Herda takes to search for her friend named Kay, who has been kidnapped by da vicked fairy, da Snow Qveen. Herda meets many obstacles in her trek before she faces a final decisive battle with the Snow Qveen. But Herda's loyal heart overcome all the adversities in this touching story of great love, human kindness, and faithfulness to one's duty. No true Russian would be critical of da Snow Qveen since she is part of our great cultural heritage."

Sybil and her companions were not quite sure what to make of the general's reference to the Snow Queen in reference to either Sybil or Russia, but they were indeed impressed by the might, power, and intimidation embodied in the stolid old soldier and represented in the headquarters building. The doors were open up and down the hallways to reveal banks of computers, masses of filing cabinets which bespoke a fearsome keeping of records about a highly submissive populace, and an army of analysts and other functionaries who leapt to attention as the general and his guests passed by their offices. Sybil, Raza, and Milton were more than surprised at how openly Gen. Mitrokhin flaunted what must have been very secret rooms, equipment, and officials. The desire to impress and to intimidate the Americans must have trumped the need to keep the secret work being done in the SVR headquarters secret.

There was no difficulty in locating the room next to the general's private office where Ed Simonsen had told Sybil that the most valuable computer information was stored. The number and seriousness of the guards was a dead giveaway—no camaraderie there. The difficulty the security precautions in that room posed seemed insurmountable for Sybil's main purpose for being in the building that day. Shades of Kim Philby and his fears: Sybil Norcroft was tasked with taking the most serious risk of her life. She shuddered to think what would become of her, of her husband and little girl, for that matter, if she were to be caught in the act of placing her USB flash drive into one of those menacing computers.

Sybil drove such thoughts out of her mind and focused on what she had to do. She despaired of ever getting into that room, let alone obtaining the thumb drive full of vital information.

"*Think, girl, think!*" she said over and over to herself.

As they walked about and Gen. Mitrokhin's monotonous loud voice droned on extolling this or that virtue and accomplishment of his country and its clandestine service, Sybil's mind raced through a dizzying series of plots and schemes—none of them worthy of a second thought. The general began making references to how hungry he was and how wonderful the food in the headquarters cafeteria was. Lunchtime and the end of the tour was looming. She had to do something. She had to do it in the next few minutes or leave in failure. Sybil Norcroft, M.D., Ph.D., F.A.C.S. abhorred even the thought of failure.

"*Failure is not an option; failure is not an option!*" she thought; and the phrase became a mantra; but for the life of her, she could not come up with a viable plan.

The tension was getting to her. She struggled to keep the stress she was feeling off her face. She needed a plan. She wanted to get out of there. She wanted to be back in the woods around Washington D.C. with Charles and Cerisse.

The SVR general was saying something about the security system of the building, something about the major renovations that had been done by his administration to survive earthquakes, bombs, and fires.

Fires! That was it! On the wall between the general's office and the secure computer room was a fire alarm which required only that a small handle be tripped to sound a general alarm that would require evacuation of the headquarters building. How to pull on that handle without being seen and drawing fatal attention to herself? Sybil looked around, her eyes frantic, as the minutes slipped away before she would no longer have access to the area.

She spied a door with the outline figure of a woman—the universal ladies restroom symbol—and the solution to her problem flashed into her mind.

"General, pardon me, but could you direct me to the ladies room? I have to powder my nose."

The ridiculous euphemism struck the general, his aide, and her two companions as funny, and caused a short moment of laughter. Everyone else, including the general, agreed that it was a good time to "ease their springs" as the general put it.

Sybil waited until the men disappeared into the men's lavatory, then she darted to the opposite wall and tripped the fire alarm handle. She just made it into the women's restroom before the screaming siren and nerve-jangling bells of the alarm rattled the walls of the building. She stepped into an enclosed booth and squatted with her feet on the toilet seat as the sound of running feet turned into the controlled noise of an army marching away from her hiding place. When the sound of the now orderly evacuation began to die down, she quietly left her perch and walked to the restroom door.

It seemed to be quiet out there in the hallway. She opened the door a crack and ventured a look out into the hallway. It was empty. She opened the door enough to be able to look into the secure computer room. No one was there! She could hardly believe her luck. Her desperate plan was working!

Sybil removed her two USB flash drives from her skirt pocket and walked calmly to the open door of the room. Her luck was holding. There was not a soul in the room. It was cool in there—obviously to protect the computers. She swiftly moved to the two largest computers, fumbled a little until she could be sure of the USB port and a little more as she forced her shaking fingers to work for her. Finally, she was able to insert the flash drives and to begin the agonizing five minute wait while the marvelous little information vacuums did their spy work. She absently wondered as she waited if this was how Kim Philby must have felt during his last agonizing hours of waiting to escape from the dragnet that was after him in Great Britain. She returned to the office door and peered out into the hall. No one.

The digital numbers on her watch crept very very slowly up. Three minutes more; two minutes more; one minute more. She literally counted down the seconds. One more peep into the hall. Still no one. Finally, the five minutes were up; and Sybil hurriedly removed the USB drives and stuffed them into her pocket. She screamed inwardly at herself to calm down and to move with caution. She wanted to run for dear life down the hallway, down the stairs, across the lobby, and out into the safe fresh air.

But, she did not do that. She was the picture of control as she stepped out into the hallway. No one was there; so, she ran down to the stairway. She could hear the tramping of feet descending the stairs off in the distance. She took the stairs two at a time being careful not to fall. On the second floor she finally came up to the backs of some of the slower evacuees and slowed down to join them. They were talking and laughing as they descended the last set of stair steps. It was apparent that none of them believed that there was a real emergency. It would be a good excuse to get outside and to take a smoke break.

Out on the lawn, there were several hundred people milling about and waiting for instructions. Sybil swung her head from side to side trying to see Gen. Mitrokhin's conspicuous grey maned head or Raza's expensive coiffure. The first one of her companions she saw was Milton Armstrong who was surrounded by a small crowd of people who were obviously very interested in whatever he was saying. Sybil walked in a zigzag pattern but as quickly as she could without drawing attention to herself. Gen. Mitrokhin and Raza were on the opposite side of the group of people with whom Gen. Armstrong was talking; and, although, they were obviously looking for her, they were faced away from her at the moment.

She unobtrusively insinuated herself into the gathering throng around the U.S. Surgeon General and pretended a rapt interest in what he was saying. Her heart was pounding so loud, and her breath was so ragged that she could scarcely make out anything he was saying. She was no more than five feet away from him when the SVR director and Raza turned her way and saw her. She feigned surprise and gave them a small wave.

She left her place in the crowd and made her way over to the general and the media star.

"I was afraid you men got lost. I have been looking all over for you," she said, preempting the question from them.

"Ant ve tot da same thingk about you, my dear. Zuch a nuisance dese fire drills, but all ist vell, I suppose. Let's get zome lunch, vat do you zay?" the general said, relieved to have all of his charges back in his view.

His eyes had a hint of suspicion in them, but he did nothing about the feelings. Where could she have gone anyway? he thought. His suspicions faded as she and the other Americans resumed their discussions and banter with him.

Their Delta flight brought Sybil, Ed, and Milton back to JFK airport four days after the American contingent to the U.N./W.H.O. healthcare forum had left for Moscow. It was a long but restful first class flight. Ed Simonsen had a seat in the very rear coach compartment. Sybil got up to stretch her legs for a moment and passed Ed as he made his way to the lavatory nearest the first class compartment. Handing off the three flash drives was a mere brush-by event unnoticeable by anyone else.

Charles and Cerisse were waiting in the baggage area of JFK when Sybil arrived. The three of them hugged exuberantly, and Cerisse peppered her mother with questions about where she had been, what she had done, and who she had met. The precocious girl had taken it upon herself to learn everything she could about Russia, Moscow, the Kremlin, and the current members of the Russian Federation governmental elite. Sybil fielded the questions for the entire ride from JFK back home to Georgetown. Most of what she told Cerisse was an exciting rendition of the truth with all of its grandeur, pomp and ceremony. Some of what she related was outright lying, and much Sybil omitted comment on was in the category of secrets—deep and forever secrets—a fact which disturbed Sybil some. She found that she was only recently coming to grips with the reality of her life as a "secret" agent. As never before, she knew she had to compartmentalize her life and experiences. She glanced furtively at Charles to see if he was suspicious and saw nothing to indicate that she had failed to keep her covenant with her spymasters. In a way, it was easier to have secrets because that way she could avoid the stressful revelation of things that would frighten Cerisse and disturb her husband.

After settling back in at home and having a couple of days of R&R with her family—including attendance at Cerisse's school activities and two company soirees with Charles—Sybil once again resumed her work at Wolf News. She huddled with Doug Mason, her photographer, and David Kilcannon, her boss in the real world. She had a brief encrypted telephone debriefing with Andrew Dillon, the DDCIA, who was her boss in the other world—the world of shadows and secrets.

With David's blessing and overseership, Sybil and Doug produced five programs related to the United Nations forum in Moscow with strong concentration on the substantive issues of the impact of trauma on health care outcomes. Doug's digital videos and stills were—as usual—dramatic and served to elevate Wolf's audience and market share. Sybil's contribution as the voice-over made even her voice one recognized throughout the world. To her credit— at Sybil's insistence—Wolf News agreed to share all of its footage with WNN, which yielded a credit pool of markers with Raza Patel, which would undoubtedly be of inestimable value as both of their careers continued to soar.

One month after arriving back in the States, Sybil was summoned to Langley. She called the main dispatch operator at the OHB [Old Headquarters Building].

"Executive 3-6115" was the response.

"Andrew Dillon," Sybil said.

CIA operators are instructed not to direct callers to specific offices, especially not those on the seventh floor.

She had a brief conversation with DDCIA Dillon's office manager and made an appointment to see him within the week.

Chapter Nine

O n the morning of the appointment with the DDCIA, Sybil got up early and drove into the District and across the George Washington Memorial Parkway Bridge to the Virginia side of the Potomac. She arrived at her destination west of Washington DC in plenty of time—the CIA building in Langley—technically, in a part of McLean, Virginia, an unincorporated area of Fairfax County a few miles west of the District of Columbia.

She pulled into the South Gate entrance, showed her credentials to the gate guard—who checked it thoroughly even though he had seen Sybil several times during the past year— and was waved through. Following Deputy Director Andrew Dillon's directions, she drove through a beautiful, lush, green forest to the Original Headquarters Building [OHB]. She parked her vehicle with its brilliant green parking permit for the day sticker in the covered parking area for ranking officers and visitors in one of the spaces that read *Deputy Director, Central Intelligence, NCS.* Part of why she had arrived so early was to make a short detour to the OHB courtyard—at the suggestion of Ed Simonsen—so, she could see the statue of Nathan Hale. Then she walked up a short flight of stairs and into the main lobby. It was an evidence of her importance to the Company that she was met there by the DDCIA himself. Director Dillon led her to the north wall where the memorial to fallen CIA heroes was placed. On the wall, in neat rows, were engraved 102 black stars with no names. On one side of the wall of stars was an American flag and on the other a CIA flag. In the center was a book—The *Book of Honor*—with, again, 102 stars, but only 63 names.

Sybil looked at Andrew's face for answers.

Andrew said, "The others are still classified."

Sybil thought to herself, "*This is the house of secrets—the puzzle palace—after all.*"

They walked to the seventh floor—Dillon was a health-nut comparable to the physical fitness regimen Sybil imposed on herself. The DDCIA nodded to his office staff and led Sybil into his private office. They had not spoken a word since she walked into the lobby.

"Thank you for coming, Sybil. I am going to brief you in person. I want you to understand that what we will discuss is beyond top secret. For this mission, you will have an Ultra TS/SCI [Top-Secret, Sensitive Compartmentalized Information, i.e. "above Top Secret"] clearance rating with SSBI [Single Scope Background Investigation]. That should alert you to both the importance of the mission I am proposing, and its seriousness from a national security secrecy aspect. I won't lecture you, Sybil. You have proved yourself. The information your mission in Moscow produced has been nothing short of phenomenal. Now, I am going to ask something more—a mission which will strain your sense of morality."

Sybil blinked at the prospects of what she might be asked to do but otherwise maintained her usual placid expression.

"You remember that during one of our earlier discussions, I hinted at the idea of you going to the Middle-East?"

"Yes."

"At that time, we did not have all of the intelligence we needed to be certain that we had the evidence we needed to deal with the problem we see. The NSA came through for us. They intercepted cell phone traffic between a relative by marriage of two of the 5,000 Saudi princes. That is not in and of itself particularly significant, but what is significant is that both of them have been in regular and frequent contact with a man who places high on our list of terrorists and no-fly individuals. You have heard about that one in the news, no doubt— Anwar al Zawlshari, ibn Muhammad."

Sybil nodded.

"I won't bore you with all of the details of the analysts' work; but to cut to the chase, the man we are interested in is named Achmed al Wahhab. We have proof positive that he was the master-mind or at least the principle executive of the terroristic Marburg virus epidemic."

Sybil's eyebrows shot up, and her eyes riveted onto Director Dillon's.

"I thought that would get your attention. We have learned a great deal about that nice man—enough to be able to put him under surveillance and to have excellent intel about his movements and agendas. In brief, he is accessible and vulnerable."

He took note of the determined set of Sybil's eyes and jaw muscles.

"How do I fit in?" she asked.

"He is going to be the chairman of a health care forum dealing with the issues of women. Most of the members of the particular lecture series he will chair are members of the Muslim Brotherhood from Egypt; so, the moderators and the audience are stacked in favor of the rights of the Islamic religion over the rights of any outside dissenters about how women should be treated, and especially about the requirements that they be fully covered and that they undergo circumcision in even its most ghastly form. We thought this might be right up your alley.

"I'm supposed to go and face the tiger in its lair? Argue them down and provide objective truth to a self-serving patriarchy that they are monsters where it comes to their treatment of women?"

She was energized and angry.

"Easy. We have a far more worthwhile but less public solution—that could be considered to be the CIA's way."

Sybil realized that she had overreacted and made herself calm down.

"No one is going to teach the Muslim Brotherhood anything. That, however, is not to say that they cannot learn on their own; and that is where you come in. In the hierarchy of Saudi political life and in al Qaeda, Achmed al Wahhab is subordinate to his brother-in-law, Daud al Sharif ibn Saud, the Saudi prince. He was the real master mind of the epidemic and uses his position in the Saudi Ministry of Transportation to fund al Qaeda and to protect the terrorists he and others within Saudi governmental offices sponsor. For now, Daud is untouchable; we simply cannot get any useful field operation level intelligence on him. We can, however, go after Achmed. Interested?"

"Sure. What do you have in mind?"

Dillon paused for a moment to make up his mind.

Then he laconically said, "kill him."

This was the moment of truth for both Sybil and Andrew Dillon. Was she in all the way—a real fighter and spy—or was she a pretty face who facilitates a few clandestine activities without getting her hands dirty.

Her training in neurosurgery had inculcated in her a well-functioning set of mechanisms to make quick and firm decisions. Her brain could analyze the necessary algorithms in flash-time.

She decided, "I'll, do it," she said.

For the next thirty minutes Sybil and Andrew worked out the necessary details of the potential first piece of wet-work of Sybil's spy career. They both understood the risks, and both knew that there was no turning back from this point on.

National and international health care issues and two local small epidemics gave Sybil an excellent chance to keep her image before the public. The two epidemics consisted of an outbreak of pertussis/whooping cough in northern Minnesota caused by a failure of religious and politically right-wing zealots to immunize their children and a Legionnaire's Disease scare in Texas, Oklahoma, and the Central Valley of California related to inadequate hygienic practices by the woefully underpaid illegal immigrants employed by the large agri-businesses in those areas. With his stature in the agri-business community, Sybil's husband, Charles Daniels was able to make his debut as a commentator in the national media.

He enjoyed the limelight and the positive attention that he was able to convey about his own business, the Argos Daniels Mitzuki Global Company. He was disappointed when his fifteen minutes of fame was over. It had been fun to work with his famous wife, and he and their daughter Cerisse had had a great time mingling with the "snootin' groupers" of the media world, as he called them. The real disappointment came three weeks after Sybil's meeting with Andrew Dillon when she had to board a Saudia flight to Riyadh.

Sybil met Raza Patel in the King Khalid International Airport baggage area, and together they booked a limo to the city's prestigious business and residential area—Olaya, which afforded easy access to the Diplomatic Quarter, ministries, government offices, shopping and business centers—and, more importantly, to the Al Faisaliah Center and the magnificent Al Faisaliah Rosewood Hotel which dominated Al Aminyah Street. Limousines filled the entrance portico, and a stream of very well dressed people moved in and out of the hotel with their assistants and retainers. They were obviously from all over the civilized world—a veritable United Nations satellite in the Middle-East—and positively emanated the glow of money and power. Sybil and Raza recognized several of the United Nations and WHO dignitaries who have been attendance at the Moscow healthcare symposium. A few very brave paparazzi made their way through the throngs of important people and shouted entreaties for the two famous American media stars to give them a couple of prints. They were soon rousted out by the arrival of the *mutaween*—religious police—which are numerous to the point of being almost omnipresent in ultra-conservative Riyadh.

Known by locals in their very private conversations as the "Dead Center of the Kingdom", Riyadh is the most straight-laced of the Kingdom's big cities owing to the great local power of Wahhabism—the most stringent, most intolerant, harshest and most powerful sect in Islam. Riyadh is a business-only destination by determined design, boring to distraction for most Westerners. But for Sybil, the principle city of Saudi

Arabia was also the best place in the Kingdom to watch at arms-length the continuing collision of tribal Wahhabi conservatism—manned in the streets by the *mutaween*—grappling with modern technology and Western influences.

Liveried doormen helped Sybil and Raza out of their limousine and into the grand hotel. Other hotel staffers—the extremely efficient bell-hop service—swept up their bags and escorted them to the reservations desk.

"Are there just the two of you, Mr...?" the reservations attendant asked Raza.

"No," he said, "We are not a couple. Please give us separate rooms on separate floors."

"Can't be too careful about appearances here," Sybil said quietly.

Raza nodded his agreement and smiled.

Sybil found her two small bags already in her Grand Suite on the third floor when she entered the rooms. She took a quick shower, drank down a bottle of Evian Water and got herself ready for the evening's round of speeches in Prince Sultan's Grand Hall. The conference room space covers an area of nearly 50,000 square feet—the largest column-free public space in the Kingdom, with a capacity for 4,000 delegates in conference-style seating and 2,800 for banquets. The first night was a banquet fit for sultans, princes, kings, and media stars. Sybil and Raza—as the media stars—gave opening talks, largely entertaining and laced with jokes. The serious speeches were to begin the following morning.

Sybil garnered one thing of importance from her attendance at the sumptuous banquet; she met and shook hands with her quarry, Achmed al Wahhab, who lined up with a number of other Saudi dignitaries to welcome the famous duo from the news services which were considered to be infamous in the

Kingdom and other Muslim countries. She was disappointed that she would not be able to meet-and-greet the top-dog, Prince Daud al Sharif ibn Saud. She smiled to herself at her chutzpah; she had harbored a hope that she could make her debut in the world of assassins by performing a twofer.

It was not until two days later that her opportunity to encounter al Wahhab alone presented itself. She gave a good, but muted speech about the health care difficulties posed by adherence to Muslim modesty policies. She reviewed the evidence for vitamin D deficiency and other female health problems directly related to wearing of the completely covering burkas and chadors.

"Although the complete covering of the female body when she is outside is described as a safety protection for women, there have been unintended deleterious health consequences," Sybil started, well aware of the disapproving glares from the men on the stand in front of the audience. "Scientists have long recognized a causal link between failure of exposure of the body to sunshine and MS [multiple sclerosis]. MS is a serious disease of the nervous system more common in females with a first manifestation in the third and fourth decades of life. The disease causes a plethora of neurological signs and symptoms that early on wax and wane but later on become permanent and progressive with devastating loss of function.

"0.68 cases per 100,000 population were recorded in Tehran in 1989 just before the commencement of the Islamic Revolution. By 2005—sixteen years after the imposition of restrictive clothing requirements for women—the incidence had risen progressively to 4.58 cases per 100,000. The change in incidence is far more than is statistically required to be significant. It is dramatic. No other change in Iran with respect to women has been discovered by researchers. Being covered by heavy opaque drapings and being prevented from exposure to life-giving sunlight, has done serious harm to the immune systems of innocent women resulting in an increased incidence of autoimmune diseases:

Vitamin D levels in women, reported in 2011, are low and are associated with rickets, osteomalacia, and osteoporosis, high blood pressure, Type 1 diabetes, colorectal cancer, Crohn's Disease, chronic lymphocytic leukemia, lupus erythemat-osis, rheumatoid arthritis, psoriasis, gout, infertility, depression, Alzheimer's disease, and periodontal disease, to name only a few conditions that have seen increased incidence in women as a direct cause of the backward requirements placed on women by the Islamic Republic of Iran."

She concluded with a humble "thank you for the opportunity of addressing this important health-care body," and sat down.

She was well-aware that even a very carefully phrased speech would result in an angry rebuttal from the chairman of the symposium, an ardent and unbending member of the Brotherhood; and the response came immediately.

He rose from his chair at the podium table and read ver-batim from a leather bound copy of the defense of Islam by the Muslim Brotherhood with all of its English grammatical errors. He obviously was waiting for this moment.

"In the name of God the Merciful"

Statement of the Muslim Brotherhood about The Convention on the Elimination of All Forms of Discrimination Against Women (CEDAW) which violates all principles of the Islamic Sharia and the Islamic community.

The Commission on the Status of Women held a confer-ence in the period from the 4th to the 15th of March 2013 to approve a document titled (*The Convention on the Elimination of All Forms of Discrimination Against Women*), a deceptive headline that includes items which collide with the principles of Islam and its basic unanimous elements of *Qur'an* and Sunnah, destroy Islamic ethics, and seek to demolish the institution of the family, which the Egyptian constitution confirmed is the building block of the society, and hence achieve the dismantling of the community, and end to the last step of the intellectual and cultural invasion, and eliminate the privacy that preserve elements of Islamic societies and its cohesion.

It is enough to give a closer reading at these items to realize what is meant to us, and these items are:

1. Grant girls their complete sexual freedom, as well as the freedom to choose their sex and the freedom to choose their sex partners (i.e., choose to have a normal sexual relationship or atypical) with rising the age of marriage.
2. Provide contraception for adolescent girls and train them on how to use it with the legalization of abortion to abort undesirable pregnancy under the name of sexual and reproduction rights.
3. Equality between an adulterous and a wife, and equality between adultery children (outside of marriage children) and legitimate sons in all rights.
4. Granting homosexuals all their rights, protection and respect, and grant protection for women in prostitution.
5. Grant wives all the right to sue their husbands with charges of rape or harassment, and the competent authorities should grant same penalties similar to raping or harassing a stranger.
6. Equality in inheritance.
7. Replace guardianship with partnership, and fully share the roles within the family between men and women such as: spending, child care, home affairs.

8. Equal access to the marriage legislations such as: Stop polygamy, *Iddah*, mandate, and the dowry, and stop obligatory spending of man on the family, and to allow Muslim women to marry a non-Muslim and others.
9. Withdraw the authority of divorce from husbands and authorize it to judiciary and share property after divorce.
10. Cancel the obligatory authorization of the husband in: travel, work or going out or use contraception.

These are the destructive means of the institution of the family and community that calls for the return of the first medieval period.

The Muslim Brotherhood call upon rulers of Islamic countries and Foreign Ministers and their representatives in the United Nations to reject this document, and also we invite this organization to live up to the level of the pure family relations prescribed by Islam.

Also Muslim Brotherhood calls al-Azhar to act according to its leading role and to condemn this document and declare the position of Islam towards its articles, as it is the reference for Muslims.

As well we call other Islamic groups and associations to take a decisive stand against this document and the like.

We also call for women's organizations to adhere to their religion and the morals of their communities and the elements of our social life and not to be seduced by the deceptive, misleading and destructive calls for urbanization.

-The Muslim Brotherhood
Cairo: 13 March 2013
[-Source: *Muslim Brotherhood Facebook Page*]

Chapter Ten

Achmed al Wahhab rose from his chair in the audience and stepped up to a microphone. He was livid with anger and outrage at the temerity of the representative of the Great Satan—and a woman, at that—to come to Allah's holy city and criticize the Holy Religion of the Believers. Who was she to enter the Kingdom and criticize her betters, the men of Islam? He denounced Sybil's speech almost line by line. His rant carried on until the podium red-light flashed indicating that his time was up. No one from the Western world dared to stand up and to defend Sybil, not even Raza, whose beliefs were at least as strong as hers on the subject of maltreatment of women. Al Wahhab wound himself up to the point that his final closing argument was a hearty "*Allahu akhbar!*"

The meeting began to break up with very little discussion among the attendees; the mood in the great room had darkened considerably; and no one wanted to fan the flames. Sybil watched al Wahhab's exit from the front of the room with the keen eye of a hunter.

She stepped out of the same VIP exit as he did being careful not to be seen. No one else was in that hallway; so, Sybil did not have the advantage of being able to blend in with a crowd. She watched as al Wahhab walked purposefully into the men's restroom. She noted that there was no women's restroom in the same area, which came as no surprise. She had to improvise.

There was a door alongside the entrance into the men's room with a sign that read, "Authorized Personnel Only". She quickly opened it a crack, just enough to ascertain that no one was in there. She surveyed the room's contents and found what she wanted. She opened a locker and took out a heavy denim chador marked "Housekeeping" and drew it on over her head. It was hot and stuffy inside and smelled of pungent body odor. She fought back nausea. There was a mop bucket still containing grey water and a damp mop hanging from a hook on the wall. She walked out of the room, head down, and swiftly stepped over to the door to the men's room.

No one was in the hall to see her; so, she bravely pushed the door open enough to see the sinks and toilet stalls. She heard groaning coming from the last stall. She bent over and quickly checked to see if there were any men's shoes showing on the floors of the stalls. Other than the one where the groaning was coming from, there were none. She and Achmed were alone in the immaculately clean tiled room. She noted that of the toilet stalls, only one had an actual Western toilet; the others were open slit trenches, including the one where she could hear Achmed al Wahhab straining.

She thought about what to do next. Lacking a better plan, she improvised with a sudden frontal assault and pushed the toilet stall door wide open. Poor Achmed was so absorbed in his gastrointestinal misery that he did not even look up.

He snarled angrily, "Get out! Occupied!"

Sybil had moistened a cloth with chloroform as she pushed her way into the small space. She stepped to Achmed's right and clapped it over his unsuspecting face. He was already weakened by the profuse diarrhea which brought him rushing to the bathroom, and he was taken entirely by surprise. He became unconscious in a matter of seconds and slid down onto the slit trench soiling his immaculate thobe with his own excrement.

The stench was almost overpowering, and Sybil had to straighten up to control the strong urge to vomit and thereby to leave incriminating evidence. She reached under her chador and pulled out a small sealed vial of a yellow viscous liquid. Achmed was entirely unconscious which gave her time to slip on the rubber gloves which Andrew Dillon had insisted she take with her as a precaution against accidental contact with the weaponized tetradoxin—TTX, from cone snails and the Vietnamese green tree snakes.

She propped the unconscious man's head back and forced open his mouth. She broke the vial's seal and pushed on the plunger which allowed ten drops of the powerful quick acting poison to drop on his tongue. One drop would have been enough to kill a horse, but Sybil was not about to take any risks. Her only real concern was that an excessive dose might be detectable by a sophisticated forensic toxicology testing of the dead man. DDCIA Dillon had assured her that it would not be detectable, but she was in a cold sweat anyway.

Sybil did not have time to moralize or to analyze. She had killed a man in cold blood, and that was that. Now, she had to keep her wits about her and to decide what to do next. She had to get rid of the poison, the gloves, the chloroform, and the cloth that was soaked in it. She had to get the chador back to the housekeepers closet, to clean herself up; and above everything else, she had to get out of that area of the hotel. She had to get back to where the crowds of dignitaries, diplomats, and scientists were gathered; so, she could establish an alibi. Her mind was working at a fever pitch, but it was as controlled as she ever was in an emergency. Her chosen profession of neurosurgery had been full of heart clutching emergencies, and her training came into good use now.

Chapter Eleven

Sybil made sure there was no tell-tale evidence that anything but an unfortunate heart attack had claimed Achmed al Wahhab's life, then she backed out of the toilet stall and swiftly washed her face and hands to clear away the sweat. She opened the men's room exit door and looked into the hallway. She did so very quickly and saw enough to keep her from stepping out into the hall immediately. A security officer was walking past the door, far enough away to be facing in the opposite direction of where Sybil was hidden. Her heart rate rose to the danger level, and she fought to regain control.

Five interminable minutes crept by before Sybil tried again. No one was in the hall. She could not hear any footsteps indicative that somebody might be coming along another hall who could possibly turn her way. She moved the bucket and mop into the hall as fast as she was able without banging the metal bucket on a nearby wall. She ducked into the housekeeping room without being seen and started to breathe again. She used the utmost caution to remove the vial of poison, the chloroform and the now dry but scented cloth from her pocket and wrapped them all in a large wad of paper towels. She wrapped that bundle in a towel, and put the bundle into a black plastic garbage bag. She removed the chador and replaced it in the same locker from which she had borrowed it, fluffed her hair, and hoped for the best with her appearance.

She risked another glance into the hallway and stepped out into it carrying the bulky trash bag. It seemed to her to be as incongruous as if she were carrying a net bag full of heads. She was desperate to find a place to dump the bag without it being readily found by a housekeeper, security guard, or police officer. She could not carry the thing back to where the evening gowned and tuxedoed grand poobahs were gathered. To her left was a direct path back to them, and to her right was an empty hallway leading to a set of doors. She chose the right.

She heard truck traffic and the clanking of cans and machinery outside the door. Time was now against her. She decided to take a look outside and hope that she could fake her way out of a confrontation with whatever or whoever was out there. She was immediately aware of the smell of fresh garbage as she opened the door a crack. She could not hear any voices; so, she opened the door and stepped out. Men were climbing aboard the side boards of a garbage truck and securing their positions with the hand holds welded onto the truck's sides. They paid her no attention there in the shadows.

Another truck was waiting just beyond where the trash truck was making its exit. There were several partially filled plastic trash cans set up in a neat row on the edge of the loading dock. She took a quick and furtive look to see what was in the receptacles. To her profound relief, they contained black plastic bags filled to varying degrees with trash. She threw her bag into one of the least full cans and was satisfied that it looked like all the rest. Finding her bag would be like finding a needle in a stack of needles.

She returned to the hallway and did not see anyone until she was well past the men's room, and then she saw two men passing her headed for the rest room. She avoided catching their glances and moved back into the large conference room which was still brimming with conference goers. She found Raza and a group of European officials from the World Health Organization who were engaged in a vigorous debate on some subject or other.

Sybil edged her way as unobtrusively as possible into the group and feigned great interest in whatever they were talking about.

Raza became aware of her and said, "Oh, Sybil, we were just talking about whether or not it was wise or politic to have brought up CEDAW [the Convention on the Elimination of All Forms of Discrimination Against Women] here in Riyadh. Since you were the only one with the courage to do such a thing, I think we'd like to hear from the horse's mouth what led you to do it?"

"You know, Raza, I have been walking around and listening to little groups like this one discuss what I said. I did not really do it to get a rise. But I did think it was time posthumous for someone to broach the subject. Surely, none of the Muslims here really expected that the subject of their egregious treatment of women would never be brought up. I am only disappointed that there was not more discussion. I would certainly have loved to get into it with the old-boys network about FGM [Female Genital Mutilation]. That would probably have been really lively."

"My government ordered me to avoid that subject no matter what," said Walther Gabler, the WHO senior vice-president from Berlin.

"Mine, too," said Pierre Danois from France. "They were very reluctant to allow me even to come here. It would have been a shame to have missed the fireworks, I have to admit."

He had a roguish smile for Sybil who smiled back.

"I guess you were keeping a low profile, Sybil," Raza said. "I wasn't even aware that you were here."

"I have been standing here for nearly half an hour. It was very insightful. Sometimes a low profile is valuable—a lesson for you and me, Raza," she said with a knowing grin for her attractive friend and nemesis.

He laughed, "I guess I was pretty much caught up in my chest beating soliloquy and didn't even look around for such an attractive trouble maker as you."

The Europeans shook their heads affably at Raza's self-effacing statement.

On the flight back to the States, Sybil took out her iPad and watched Wolf News's replay of the furor she had caused in the ultra-conservative Saudi capital. The network showed the most flattering photos and video clips possible of her, and the commentators lavished praise about her candor and courage. She was unsure how her minders at the CIA would react to her performance and to a lesser degree how official and public Washington would perceive what she had done. They would never know what she had really done.

"*Wouldn't that be a shock to their tender little sensitivities?*" she thought, as she nodded off to sleep.

Because her trip had resulted in so much great footage—including several segments featuring Sybil with Raza Patel—

the stories were kept alive and fresh for an entire five day news cycle. The Wolf News vice-president for human resources, Gwen Packard, called Sybil into her office.

"Sybil, you are a tireless worker; and we don't want you to get exhausted or overexposed. I want you take some R&R—say a week or so—before you get back to your incredible schedule, okay?"

"What brought this on, if I may ask?"

"Well…part of it is my personal bias. I have been to Riyadh more than once, and I have to tell you the place makes my skin crawl. I'm sure you encountered those weasels, the *mutaween*?"

"The religious police."

"Yeah. Them."

She said it with a level of disdain that one could almost taste.

"I was exhausted by the time I got out of there. I stayed on Olaya Street at the Tulip Hotel—nothing like the magnificent Al Faisaliah Rosewood Hotel where you stayed. I was working for Reuters at the time. Anyway, when I first got into that nasty place, I saw two burly, angry *mutaween* thugs beating a woman with short billy clubs. She was middle-aged, a suicide blond, and was wearing a low-cut casual blouse that exposed her technologically enhanced bosoms, a decidedly foolish thing to do in Riyadh, of course. The *mutaween* were screaming at her in Arabic, which she obviously did not understand, and had reduced her to a tear-sodden shadow of her former self as her aging husband stood helplessly by. It was just one of several things I saw about how women get treated there."

"There were certainly plenty of them around the hotel," Sybil added.

"You bet. The Saudi state is absolutely beholden to the Wahhabi family, and the *mutaween* are the SA storm troopers of the "Kingdom of Hatred". The legal system there prescribes capital punishment like beheading and what other corporal punishment like even cutting off hands and feet for crimes as bad as murder and rape of an important girl, and even for such much more minor things like robbery. They also do canings and floggings; this is the twenty-first century for heaven's sake! You know there are many poor folks there who sometimes have to become robbers to live. The amputations are also for drug smuggling, adultery in women, and for being gay or lesbian. The rich ones or the royal family don't seem to get such bad punishments. I saw unfairness everywhere. The *mutaween* can even come into a person's home and arrest him or her for drunkenness. I'd like to see the day that they went into a prince's palace and arrested one of them.

"Reuters wanted me to get the straight skinny on abuses against Shi'ites by Sunnis there in Hatred's Kingdom. They tried to warn me that it wasn't a great gig for women. I could not have imagined how much of "not a great gig" it could be. First off—when I applied for a visa—I was told that I could not travel alone in the Kingdom. It made me mad, but I already knew about that. So, I went through all of the hoops to get a male companion to be with me all the time, to drive, and to be able to talk to the loonies that stop you everyplace. I had to get one of the WWN guys we do business with to sponsor me to make sure I didn't go around exposing myself or raping poor little innocent Saudi men…give me a break!

"I figured I could put up with it all, get in and get out. Was I in for an education! We landed in Riyadh and took an airport taxi into town to the Al Faisaliah Hotel. On the way into town, I read in the newspaper that they had just beheaded a guy for being a witch. This is the twenty-first century! A witch! I got out before my male companion, who is a nice guy but useless in business of getting news and about as much protection as my aunt Gertrude. This nasty little *mutaween* creep walked up behind me and whacked my ankle with a little club. Big deal, my ankle was showing. It still hurts. He made a hard grab on my butt; and the hotel doorman yelled at me not to fight back or to protest; or they would arrest me. That set the stage. Later, when I got to the foreigner's compound at the oil station, a couple of women there told me that one of the most common reasons for women to be in prison in that hell-hole of a country is because they were raped. That's it. Because *they* were raped!

"Men can marry girls younger than one year of age. Under Sharia law, they can lawfully consummate the marriage with a nine year old. That's to protect the girls, you see. Supporters of a law to ban child brides were declared to be apostates under the Sharia. Some progressives got a bill prepared to raise the marriageable age to seventeen; it was sent back to parliament where it was declared unIslamic! More than a quarter of all marriages involve girls under the age of fifteen; that's so the girl can be shaped into an obedient wife, bear more children, and be kept bare foot and pregnant and away from temptation. What crap! It's every bit as much about the money; poor fathers sell their daughters; so, the dirty old rich men can have little girl virgins to deflower. The Arab men I talked to kept telling me about how peaceful the religion is, how protective it is of women and girls who are considered so feeble-minded that they can't do business, drive a car, or handle their own sexuality.

"This nine year old business is just one of the 'protections'. In the Kingdom, the accusation of rape requires four witnesses. How often do you think four witnesses see a rape? The foreign working girls haven't got a chance. If they get raped, the only thing they can hope for is to be able to get out of the country as fast as they can; and that is not all that easy. Make an accusation, and you are more likely to do prison time than the rapist. And that is as if those poor neglected men can't get enough sex. Any man can have four wives and even one temporary wife for a year if he wants. It's heaven for men, apparently. In the tribal areas a woman can be murdered just for leaving home without permission, let alone for speaking to an unapproved man. They don't admit it, but they still practice female genital mutilation out there in the hinterlands. Most of the poor little girls die because of the filthy conditions and failure to control hemorrhage when the mutilations are done. Their mothers take them to the butchers and hold them down. You learn a lot if you listen to women. They suffer, and they pour out their hearts to a sympathetic listener.

"When I was not crying over the women and girls, I was being furious over the obstructions the men put up to interfere with my getting my job done. My degree in journalism and all my experience being embedded with the marines during Desert Storm wasn't enough. They had to have the approval of the kid who had to come with me. He didn't know the journalism business from apple butter. It was a terrible waste of time. In the end, the *dumbkopfs* just couldn't bring themselves to work with a woman.

"They are horrible bigots. I saw a bunch of Saudi National Guardsmen cut up a little group of Shi'ite pilgrims with their swords. It seems that the Saudis made it illegal to celebrate the main Shi'ite holy day, the one called Ashurah, which is a day of deep mourning for the death of one of their saints or something which occurs on the 10th of Muharram. That's some month on their old inaccurate calendar. That's the day when all those crazy people go around whipping themselves. Anyway, I saw. I mean—*I saw myself*—that they killed some of those poor fools. That was it for me. I called the news consortium and got myself out of there as fast as transportation could make it happen.

"I tell you, as soon as I got off the plane at JFK, I went out to a greasy spoon and ate a ton of bacon and had pork roast dinners with wine every day for a month, drove my car across the U.S. all by myself, and pranced around half naked every time I got back to my own little apartment. The day I got back to America and kissed the ground was the best day of my life so far. I was out of Saudi Arabia."

"I'm an outspoken feminist," Sybil said, "I probably wouldn't last long there."

"No probably about it," Gwen said. "But I've been prattling. Take the time to wash the taste of that anti-woman place out of your mouth. I'll see you bright and early next Monday. Now shoo."

Sybil thought about her next utterance for a moment or two before asking, "Am I in the dog-house? Have I done something that has displeased the grand poobahs of Wolf News? Is that why you want me out of here?"

She was fishing for a hint that her poorly received talk about the treatment at the Riyadh meetings was the subject of criticism behind closed doors on the upper floors of Wolf News HQ.

"Good heavens, no. Whatever made you think such a thing? As the head of HR, I shouldn't tell you this, but the bean counters told me that your coming to Wolf has added just over eleven million dollars to the pot, and you haven't been here a year. You could name your price, and they'd pay it to keep you. Don't you dare ever tell anyone I said that. I would deny it, but they'd can me in a minute if they thought it was true."

She was all smiles as she said it, but Sybil figured there was more than a grain of truth in what the head of HR was saying. She promised to keep mum—another little secret to put away in her file.

Chapter Twelve

Sybil left V-P Gwen Packard's office and flew to Reagan National Airport where she had left her car. The first thing she did was to drive to Charles's office and climbed the 13 flights of stairs to his office. It felt good. She was amused that, even in modern and jaded New York, there was no 13th floor.

She asked Charles's office manager, Doris Duncan, if he was in.

"He is. He's on the phone for the moment. I'll let him know you're here, Mrs. Daniels, as soon as he can talk. Have a seat."

Sybil seldom heard herself referred to as "Mrs. Daniels", and she rather liked it. The change of her name to his had bothered her at first, but she grew to like it because it afforded her anonymity when she wanted to have it. That was particularly useful now that she was so much in the public eye. Charles had never pushed the issue and would have been perfectly all right if she had insisted on her right as a feminist to keep her own name or to hyphenate their two names. Nonetheless, it had pleased him considerably that the "Snow Queen" to the rest of the world was willing to make the concession to be merely, "Mrs. Daniels" among their friends and associates.

"He'll see you now," Mrs. Duncan said. "Walk right in."

"To what do I owe this pleasure?" Charles asked and caught her up in a fervent embrace.

"Just out slumming," Sybil replied snuggling closer to his chest.

"How come you're not at work? Get fired?"

"Nope, rewarded. They told me to take the week off and go away. I want us to do just that. How about a quick car trip?"

"Really?"

He looked at her with a theatrically quizzical expression, one eyebrow raised.

"Who are you? Who has taken over my wife's body?"

Sybil laughed, "Silly, I mean it. Get off work early and let's go tonight."

"Where?"

"I have never been to the Crazy Horse Monument or even to Mount Rushmore. I want to take Cerisse there. There is so much great stuff to see in America; let's get started while we're young."

"I'm feeling younger by the minute, Mrs. Daniels. Why don't you arrange things with Cerisse's school. I should be back home by five, and we can pack up and head out."

"I'll get on-line and find us some one-night cheap hotels."

"The ones we reach through certain half-deserted streets, the muttering retreats of restless nights in one-night cheap hotels, and sawdust restaurants with oyster shells?"

"Aren't you the English major, now? Mrs. Hoyt from senior English would be surprised that she did at least get something into my head to know *The Love Song of J. Alfred Prufrock* well enough that you can't snow me," Sybil laughed as she walked out of his office with a backward wave and a smile.

Cerisse was thrilled. She loved America and all of its quirkiness and her parents who could just take off on a lark. South Dakota, the four faces on the mountain, the colossal partly carved Indian face, the open prairies and the wild creatures roaming the vastness of America were inspiring and thrilling to the little girl. She was having more experience and more good days in the last few months than she had accumulated in a lifetime.

Charles and Sybil had never enjoyed life so much before and asked each other how they had lived without seeing the wonder on a child's face every day. Sybil concentrated on the idyllic road tour and worked on not thinking about Achmed al Wahhab's face. She also worked on not thinking about what she would have to do next. DDCIA had hinted broadly that it would be worse than Saudi Arabia.

Sybil received a call on her iPhone at six o'clock in the morning from a source identified only as "Code Company". She was inclined to ignore it as just another one of those annoying advertising calls. There was a difference between this identifier and any other she had seen. It flashed insistently and would not go away even when she tried to turn off her phone.

"Hello?" she said tentatively.

"Norcroft?" the voice replied.

"Yes, what is this about?"

"Are you on a secure line?"

"No."

"Then come to the office in person. It is urgent."

The caller hung up leaving Sybil to try and decide if it had been a prank call of some sort or if it was genuine. If it was genuine, then what was it about? What office? Why in person? She decided that it must mean the "Puzzle Palace— Langley", and the office referred to must be that of the DDCIA, Andrew Dillon.

"What's going on, Sybil?" Charles asked.

"I'm not sure. Something at Wolf. They said it's urgent; so, I have to catch the first flight to the city."

He groaned and turned over to finish his night's sleep. Sybil felt uncomfortable about having told Charles an outright lie, the first time in their married life that she had ever done so. In the compartmentalized world of secrets where she lived without her husband and daughter, it seemed right and logical. She was not sure she would ever get used to that schism with which she had to live.

She risked appearing foolish by just showing up at Dillon's office without calling and left after a five minute spit bath for Langley. Her presumption that Dillon had summoned her was confirmed when she was ushered through the main gate by the guard who was obviously expecting her.

She got a visitor's pass and a guard as a guide and climbed the stairs to the seventh floor of the OHB. Dillon's secretary was all business and took her directly into the DDCIA's office.

"Good morning, Sybil. Forgive me for the cloak-and-dagger stuff on the phone."

"I'm just glad I could figure it out and come to the right conclusion."

"You're smart. I knew I wouldn't have to go through a Dick-and-Jane routine. This is serious and secret. One thing I realized is that I had not provided you with the most basic of spy tools now that you are part of the smoke-and-mirrors team. So, belatedly, here is a black credit card; its limit is eleven trillion dollars, but you have to account for everything you spend. It never expires unless you are no longer with the Company. And here is the world's best cell phone. It works everywhere on earth and is simple to use. You just push this button, and you connect with the only number you can call—the secure switchboard here in the OHB [Old Headquarters Building]. This is your code identifier. Memorize it. If you must keep a copy, don't indicate what it is, and hide it in the most secure place you can devise—like under a floor board in your office, that sort of thing. It seems melodramatic, but your life and our missions depend on the sanctity of the code being used only by you."

The code was simple: S7A3N0D75#Marburg. The letters were her initials; the numbers were her birthdate—July 30, 1975, and Marburg was her main claim to fame with the CIA.

"Got it," she said.

"And finally, here are your keys to the executive washroom."

He handed over a CIA identification card in a new leather cred pack. The credentials actually had a gold plated badge with the letters "CIA" across the top, and the numbers "73075" at the bottom—which Sybil presumed was her easily remembered Company personnel record number—beneath the formal "Special Agent" identification. She liked the way it looked and how easily it fit into her purse.

Lastly, he gave her an official CIA agent tag on a lanyard. She would no longer have to wear a VISITOR pass which so lacked built-in value of the designation of being one of those who belonged.

"Unfortunately, Sybil, you will have to hide those things in your secure place for your next mission. You will be going to Paris, and you won't be an official CIA special agent while you are there. Quite the contrary. You did so well on your two previous missions for the Company, you are becoming type cast. We have another assassination for you. It is one you may well relish despite the departure from your normal self. The target is Daud al Sharif ibn Saud, the Saudi prince. I think you are well aware of him and his role in life."

"I know something about him—just what you told me—but why Paris and why now?"

"I'm glad you didn't ask, 'why me?' No one is forcing you to take any wet-work assignment, but I hope you can consider what I am about to say as a compliment; you are very good at it; and you are in a perfect position to pull it off without being suspected."

"I guess I have set aside my conscience. What a far cry from my persona of just a couple of years ago. It seems unreal, like something out of Hollywood. But, I do believe it is the only way to deal with those mass murdering terrorists. This is almost personal. I found that I could focus on the mission and not be diverted, and I can ignore my conscience to get it done. I guess you could say that I *am* good at it."

"But, I have to say, not good enough. We are asking you to do things for which you lack the skill set. We must correct that deficiency forthwith, Sybil. You need to do some serious training—three months' worth of serious training with regular refresher courses. Originally, I saw you as a sort of graduate level analyst, then as a perfectly positioned pawn to allow the agents to get an operation into place. I have changed my mind, and Ed Simonsen agrees; you are a natural field agent, a capable assassin who needs to learn and to hone life-saving and mission effective skills. That's a lot to take in. Can you do it?"

"I have thought a lot about it. Could I lie to people, compromise them, betray them, and even kill them in the interests of my country's national security? With two missions under my belt, the answer has been 'yes'. But there is a practical problem. I have no argument about secrecy and security, but it will be impossible to live completely a lie with my husband. He is too intelligent to accept a series of prevarications about why I am going away yet again and for long periods. I can't get away with the charade that I will be on assignment for Wolf News and incognito. He won't buy it, and he has considerable information gathering resources of his own that he could use to find me and to get a reasonably plausible handle on what I am doing. I need your permission to include him into the small circle of individuals who know that I am an agent of the CIA and that I will have to be away for periods without explanation."

She looked at the DDCIA earnestly. She was unemotional, but her argument was a sound one, and could not be ignored.

"Ummh, Sybil, that's a tough one. Usually we have field agents without such serious personal involvements. We prefer orphans and recluses generally. Charles would have to be vetted thoroughly. He will have to agree—subject to severe penalties for failure—to keep it an absolute secret that you are a Company agent. You can talk to him; and I will talk to him; but we will both have to tread lightly, agreed?"

"Yes, Sir."

She felt a huge sense of relief. That out of the way, Andrew laid out the plans for her mission in France.

When she understood the mission, its objective and the ways that were being put into place to accomplish it, Andrew added a new requirement for her.

"You are going to have to train, and train seriously. You will have to enter the Camp Peary formal program for ninety days during which you will be entirely out of contact with your work and your family. No one can know where you are or what you are doing. Charles can know that you are on CIA business and nothing more. There is something of a time crunch. Hard as it may be to pull off, you need to start the training first of next month. Daud al Sharif ibn Saud will be in Paris to meet with a consortium of Islamic charities to arrange financing for one or maybe several complex attacks against the U.S. He will be there for five days, and that is the only foreseeable window of opportunity to bring him down. You will need everything we can provide, and you will have to be a very capable and resourceful black-ops agent to do it. His security is the equal of anyone's in the world."

Over the next week, Sybil organized her tasks, attacking the most difficult one first—as she always did. She broached the subject of her involvement with the CIA with Charles using every tactic she knew about to mollify him into acceptance. She made a date with him and made all of the arrangements: dinner at Masa, the Japanese restaurant in the Time Warner Center. She used all of her media celebrity to secure one of the highly sought after seats. There are only 26 seats in the restaurant, and there is no menu. The dinner—an unequaled omakase experience—lasted for three hours. Afterwards, she took him to the penthouse suite in the Marriott Marquis Hotel and seduced him.

When he was thoroughly surfeited and weakened, she dropped her bombshell. He gave her the perfect segue.

"Okay, Sybil, what's up? I have just been introduced into the delights of the world's most accomplished courtesan. Tell me what this is going to cost."

She laughed and snuggled up to him seductively.

"Not that much. Just to listen to something I have to tell you and promise that you won't interrupt or get mad until I finish."

"Uh oh."

"Promise," she said and snuggled some more.

"How can I resist," he said admitting complete surrender.

She then told him as much as she had been told she could by DDCIA Dillon. She was clear about being a full-fledged CIA special agent, but nothing about the nature of her assignments. She made it clear that she never could tell him, and he would just have to trust her. He listened impatiently, but quietly.

"You can never tell anyone, Charles. In fact, you are going to have to become a very good liar, like I am. I know that it is alien to your nature, but what I am doing is important. It was hard to get my superiors at the Company to agree, and to do so I had to promise that you would allow yourself to be vetted for a classified security clearance. Please do that for me. We can work together on this to that limited degree, if you will."

He laughed at how well she had outmaneuvered him but agreed to her heartfelt request. It cost her another seduction, a price she enthusiastically paid with interest.

Next, she arranged a meeting with David Kilcannon and Gwen Packard in David's office at Wolf News. She told them that she needed a three month sabbatical to clear her slate and her mind for several projects she was working on. They could tell the world that she was going to Paris for a meeting of the

World Health Organization where it was to be announced that she had been selected to serve on the supreme council as a member/consultant for a three year term. During the visit to France, she would be working with a consortium of healthcare experts on a plan for the United States healthcare delivery that could possibly help correct some of the grievous flaws in the current plan—the PPACA—which was passed into law in October, 2010 and had failed to live up to almost any of its much vaunted expectations. The network could be as public as it wanted during her stay in France. She asked that they arrange for a collaborative effort with Raza Patel and WWN for the project.

They agreed, but they asked dozens of questions about what she would be up to for during the three month sabbatical. She was adamantly evasive, and they finally gave up and acquiesced. Were it not for her fame and all of the income she had produced for the network during her period of working for Wolf, neither executive would have given her request a second thought before turning her down.

A week later she arrived at Camp Peary, Virginia to begin her training. She had been doing aerobics training for several months, and felt like she was in good enough condition to do the physical part of the training fairly easily. That was the first revelation she had coming.

The alarm bell rang at 0400 on the day after she arrived and settled in. She hurried to dress and get ready for physical training. She was the last in line when the ramrod stiff middle-aged military appearing trainer took his place in front of the assembled agents whose identities were all secret and phony as three-dollar bills.

"This is not the military, and this is not boot camp," he said. "It's worse. You are all pretty old for this kind of thing, and you are going to hurt. No one will call you names or demean you. You can quit whenever you want; just whisper in my ear. Don't ask questions of other people. If you do, I will whisper loudly in your ears; and you will go home or worse. You don't need to know why anyone else is here, and they don't need to know a thing about your business. You will have the same routine every day: up at 0400, do an hour of aerobics training—read, running—then have 30 minutes for breakfast and a shower. At 0600 you will assemble on the mats in the gym for martial arts training. That is going to hurt, and you are not going to whine. If you break something, you will get appropriate care; and you may, or may not, get to come back to try again. Lunch is at noon sharp. At 1230 you will assemble at the shooting range for two hours. Then you will all go your separate ways for the specialized instruction for which you have been sent here. Questions?"

There were none. There were fifteen candidates in all, eleven of which were cocksure young men who appeared to be in top physical condition. Sybil presumed they were of recent or even current military backgrounds. No one looked soft or to be out of condition. Sybil's competitive spirit was challenged.

At the end of the obstacle course run, her legs were rubber; and her heart was thundering in her chest. She was a sweaty mess. Only two of the young cocksure men were still cocksure. They were all ravenous and gobbled down a huge breakfast of cooked cereal, eggs, breakfast meats, whole-grain bread, and fruit. Sybil observed that no one smoked; it would have been well-nigh impossible to have bad habits and survive the rigors of the training.

That was driven home by the three hours on the mat. The first day was spent in seeing who had skills and who did not; and more importantly, who could still stand up willing to go on with the rest of the day despite pain in every muscle and joint. Every candidate fought at least four MMA matches. Sybil lost every match and received no sympathy, nor did she receive any insults or derision. Two of the cocksure young men whispered in the drill master's ear before lunch and were never seen again.

Lunch was equally as hearty as the breakfast had been. Sybil pounded in the protein to keep up her strength. She was angry with herself for having been such a wuss during the martial arts training and made a vow that she would be the best "man" in the units before her three months was up. Her afternoon was spent shooting a variety of weapons on the range with a special accent for her to become facile with the use of several sniper rifles, an assortment of handguns to determine the one that would be best for her, knife fighting and throwing, and bomb making and defusing.

In the classroom, she began to learn the rudiments of trade craft, and Sylvia was fascinated and recharged by the intellectual stimulation. The subjects were demanding: computer hacking, encryption, decryption, case histories with a moral and a message, and disguises. Before leaving the classroom for another hour of physical exercise, she was issued a packet with three full fake but very genuine appearing identities, including one French passport in the name of someone she had never heard of but looked exactly like her.

The next morning, there were only 12 members who lined up to start day two. No one was cocksure then. The lesson had been learned. Surprising to her, Sundays were days off; and the candidates were forbidden to exercise or to read or study the information they were learning in the classroom. A day of rest and relaxation was a requirement.

For the next three months, the sophisticated and well-toned professional woman who arrived at Camp Peary gradually became a taut, quick, strong fighter with a new set of skills that would match the prowess of the vast majority of men in the world, in or out of the military. She became a master at Brazilian Jiu Jitsu and IDF [Israeli Defense Forces] krav maga, and an expert knife fighter and bomb maker. Her intelligence came to the fore as she digested a great mass of trade craft. By her last day, she could cope with computers, encryptions, was an expert sniper markswoman, and could do escape and evasion procedures with a flare. Her natural resourcefulness was her best attribute, and her drill master and classroom instructors gave the DDCIA glowing reports.

Chapter Thirteen

Sybil flew by Air France to Orly International Airport in Paris. The flight was pleasant and restful. The French still served meals on board unlike the uncivilized Americans; and in First Class, the American celebrity-cum-spy dined like a princess. A talkative cabbie drove her to her hotel— *L'Ermitage Sacre Couer* on the Rue Lamarck, Montmarte. She showed her passport and checked in to a suite. The hotel was a small but beautiful and elegant hill-top mansion-turned-guesthouse, a classy bed-and-breakfast place. Her room had been booked as a "face Basilica"— *Basilique Sacré-Coeur*—view, as opposed to the less expensive and less exclusive "face Paris" view. She was on the second floor in the only room left available for such a prominent guest.

All twelve of the rooms in the family-owned B&B were artistically-minded guestrooms. Each room was papered with English flower-print fabrics and furnished with handcrafted beds, armoires, tables, and cut glass lamps dating from the early 1900s. Each room had a slightly different décor; but all were designed to charm even the most finicky guest; and Sybil felt at home in hers.

The guest-house's nod to the modern man—at least in Sybil's room—was deep plush synthetic French-made wall-to-wall carpeting. The carpet was so soft that she made no sound as she crossed to set her bags on the luggage holder under the window. The room—like the hotel—was otherwise simple: no TV, no elevator, and no smoking. All rooms were equipped with standard tiled bathrooms, hers with a blue and grey design of French countryside silhouettes. There was a narrow shower—i.e., a French shower—and even a bathtub—white, small, and with gold claw-feet holding it well off the floor that was clean to the point of sterility. Her window—which provided a breath-taking vista centered on the Basilica of the Sacred Heart—opened onto a small terrace to which was attached one of the few outside fire escapes. It was good to be in what the French called "civilization" in the most civilized city on the planet.

She napped until three-thirty then shook off the rest of her jet-lag and got ready for her first round of talks in the Paris World Health Summit. The topic of that afternoon and evening's meeting was to receive the annual report from the Secretariat to the WHO's Governing bodies on the progress made on monitoring of WHO's adherence to the Paris Declaration on Aid Effectiveness. It was Sybil's responsibility to refine and to articulate a clear approach to cooperation and harmonization at the country-country level. That she spoke French like a native was a decided plus.

The first presenter was Daud al Sharif ibn Saud from Saudi Arabia representing the world-wide Consortium of Muslim Charities, a multi-billion dollar charity organization which provided education, construction of mosques with small emergency clinics, and humanitarian aid to Muslims. Sybil knew what the rest of the members of the WHO leadership seated around the huge oval conference table did not know. The charity used only 20% of the funds garnered from the faithful for the stated purposes. Even the stated purposes were exclusive, and Sybil bristled at that. However, the information furnished her by the analysts at the CIA told her that the other 80% went to further terrorism in every country in the world.

His presentation was succinct and highly polished. He had given it several hundreds of times and was successful in raising 7% more funds every year. This accounted for about the same increase in terrorist attacks each year since he took the reins of the Consortium. The CIA showed Sybil the net worth of the Consortium—$14.8 billion, and the record of deaths inflicted through the use it its funds—6,239 in the past eight years when the Company began maintaining surveillance on the "charity" foundation. Back at Langley, she had had an opportunity to examine the evidence that ibn Saud was a very well positioned terrorist, acting through his brother-in-law, Achmed al Wahhab, late of al Qaeda.

There was a reception afterwards, and Sybil got to meet the renowned humanitarian—and terrorist—in a reception line for major personal contributors to the Paris World Health Summit. There were ten contributors in the line and 63 WHO officers to meet-and-greet them. Sybil shook his hand. There were a dwindling number of WHO officers coming along; so, they did not have to hurry. His hand lingered a touch too long on hers then he gripped it with both of his hands.

"You are a lovely as well as a brilliant young woman, Dr. Norcroft. I missed meeting you when you were in my country and am happy to be able to do so now. Perhaps we will have an opportunity to get together on a more private basis sometime during our mutual stay in the City of Lights. Maybe dinner?"

She wanted to recoil; but instead, she ignored his eyes which were focused on an area about six inches below her clavicles, and said—with a flash of inspiration—"that would be most pleasant, Mr. ibn Saud."

"Please call me Daud. My friends do. May I call you Sybil?"

"Of course. It is more intimate and friendly," she replied and gave him a sloe-eyed look directly into his obsidian eyes for a moment—enough to convey a small discrete message but not enough to convey a woman-to-man challenge which she knew would turn him off.

Back in her room, she called Ed and Andrew on the CIA satellite phone and reported on the contact.

"So, you think he came on to you?" the DDCIA asked.

"Definitely."

"That should abbreviate things, Sybil, but be ever so careful. He is a snake. He likes to hurt women. Our dossier has some scary incidents described in it."

"I will," she said; and they got down to the business of making a plan.

It was obvious that she would never get by his security staff carrying a gun. She would have to walk past a portable metal detector; so, a regular knife was out of the question. He did not drink alcohol and had a hard and fast rule about ever drinking from an unsealed container like a cup, a tumbler, or a flute. It would be impossible to put a drug in a drink or to apply a drug to his person because she would not be able to slip on latex gloves as she had done when she dispatched his brother-in-law Achmed al Wahhab. It was Ed who came up with a solution.

Sybil and Daud did not encounter each other the next day or the next after that until he sought her out in the private U.N. officials' lounge.

"We meet again, my dear," he said smoothing the passage of words with a fine and practiced application of oil.

He was acting as if it was an accidental encounter.

"And, how nice it is. Please…take a seat by me; so, we can talk. Tell me about yourself," she cooed in her best practiced courtesan patter.

He sat and somehow his silk thobe covered arm managed to brush her chest. He looked at her to see if she was going to take umbrage, but she smiled at him.

"I do have a pressing meeting, and I am sure you are tired. Perhaps you could have a restorative nap and a shower, and we could meet in my suite in Le Meurice—say ten tonight? I am at my best in the late evening and my worst in the morning. I hope you are not, how do you say? a morning person, Sybil."

"I am not a morning person which has always made my life difficult, Daud," she lied, "But perhaps tonight that will be an advantage."

The rather innocuous words she said were innocent enough, but the way she said them was turgid with innuendo, especially with her smoky sloe-eyed look.

He bit hard.

"Not to be presumptuous, but could I have my driver pick you up at nine-forty-five?"

"That would be lovely, Daud," she said with promise and a bit of naughtiness in her cultured voice.

They were speaking French which accentuated the words, the thoughts, and the moment.

As soon as she got back to her hotel room, Sybil called Ed using their secure phones.

"Ed, we don't have much time. The target was made a move on me. He wants to have a driver pick me up for a candle-light and roses rendezvous dinner in his room at Le Meurice. I need a set of ultra-sexy undies—garter belts, mesh thigh-high stockings, suspenders, skimpy-lacy stuff. The garter belt has to be wide enough to hide the ceramic knife. Please get some of our big guys as close to ibn Saud's room as possible. It is likely to get very dicey once the action starts. I am not at all sure that I can con the guards into leaving his front door. I need a dark brunette wig and a change of clothes to a black hoody, tights, and running shoes. Have a car ready at a moment's notice. I will probably have to go out by a rear exit. Watch for me."

"You don't have to do this, Sybil. We can get him another time, another way."

"No we can't. You know that. He is as careful and elusive and mean as a wolverine. He will keep on killing for years if we don't stop him tonight. I can't stand to be on the same earth as that monster. No cold feet, Ed. We have to do this, and we have to do it right."

"All right, Sybil. Safety first. I will have a hair trigger on my impulses to come after you."

"Thanks, Ed, but give me a reasonable chance to get the job done."

Sybil was physically uncomfortable in the constricting undergarments Ed purchased. She was socially and emotion-ally uncomfortable in the low-necked evening dress he got for her as well. Although it was a fairly warm evening, she put on an expensive grey silk lace shawl to cover her when she was in public. She felt conspicuous waiting beside the revolving doors just inside *L'Ermitage Sacre Couer*. She knew that it wouldn't matter if people did look at her. The brunette wig Ed had found was perfect. It was in a Dutch cut and changed her looks so dramatically that her husband would not have recognized her in a casual passing.

"*If only Charles could see me now*," she thought.

Daud ibn Saud's Mercedes limousine pulled up to the curb, and the driver got out and opened the rear passenger door for her. The limo was almost exactly the color of her shawl.

"*What a nice fashion touch*," she thought and hurried to the open door.

Although she felt like a nudist at a nun's convention, no one paid any attention to her. Elegant women wearing less than her floated around the lobby of Le Meurice, lightly holding onto the forearms of equally elegant men twice their age. None of them seemed the least bit self-conscious; so, Sybil put on her game face and avoided looking down at her chest.

Daud ibn Saud and his retinue—including three wives and eleven children—occupied four large rooms on the ninth floor. There were two guards stationed in front of the largest suite, which Sybil surmised was ibn Saud's.

The driver stopped in front of that door and nodded to the guards.

He spoke to Sybil for the first time then, "Do not worry, Madam; the guards are here to protect you. The family and their guards are out to a performance of *Cirque du Soleil* and will be gone all evening. This entire floor is secure."

For some reason, that did not really make Sybil feel better.

The guards were apologetic about having to do so, but patted her down thoroughly. She recognized that they were professionals—no Russian hands or Roman fingers.

As she walked into the lavish suite, Daud motioned her forward and the guards back out of the room.

"I have some lovely fruit punch, compliments of the hotel," he said. "As you no doubt know, I am a devout Muslim and do not partake of spiritus frumenti."

"Of course," she lied, "neither do I."

Daud's face eased into a smile of acceptance.

Sybil did not allow her face to register her opinion of his hypocrisy—*won't take a sip of good wine, but will be an active adulterer and a murderer.*

"Perhaps you would like to join me in my quarters. I have some lovely *object de arte* you might find interesting," Daud said suppressing a lewd grin.

Sybil smiled, suppressing amusement; he might just as well have given her a rendition of oil-can Harry inviting a shy damsel into his room to see his etchings.

"I would love to," she said.

To her surprise, he was a gentleman—no rushing, no leering, no crude remarks. He did quite obviously appreciate her décolletage. She began to relax.

"You are lovely, Doctor. What a charming combination of beauty and brains you are!"

"Thank you, Daud. You are a fine specimen of a man yourself. I would like to hear more about you. You have an amazing reputation in the humanitarian world."

"How nice it is to have a woman want to know about me. Beautiful women are usually quite boring, always wanting to talk about their interests and to ignore the man. They always want something, unlike you. I am impressed; and, if you don't mind me saying so, quite taken with you."

"The feeling is mutual. Does it seem warm to you, Daud? I would like to remove my shawl, if you don't mind."

"Certainly not. Let me help you."

His fingertips caressed her bare shoulders but went no further. She noticed that he winced with a momentary muscle spasm.

"You seem to be having some pain, Daud. I hope it is nothing serious."

"It's nothing. I just worked out a bit too hard today. I am not as young as I once was."

"Nonsense. Would you like me to massage your sore back and arms?"

He could hardly believe his luck. It was going to be easier than he thought.

"That would be wonderful. I have some massaging cream. If you don't mind, I will go get some and change into something more appropriate."

"Good idea. Perhaps you have a robe I could wear. I don't want to get any greasy lotion on my dress."

The mention of her dress caused his eyes to focus below her clavicles once again.

"I'll fetch one. You can slip out of your dress behind the dressing shield there."

He left the room, and Sybil hurriedly extricated the razor sharp double-edged ceramic knife from her garter belt. It was ivory white, the same color as her lace underwear and the sheets on the overly large king size bed. She raced to the bed and hid the knife under the pillow. Daud returned in less than a minute dressed in an oriental robe that opened in the front. It was made of ornate black silk. He handed the terry cloth robe to Sybil. She made an effort to let him get a subtle eyeful as she slipped out of her dress and put on the robe.

Chapter Fourteen

"Daud, that robe looks like it will make your back inaccessible. We're adults, why don't you slip out of it, and I will put a towel over you; so, the interesting parts are out of sight. That way, I can do a proper job."

He fumbled around under the bed sheet and handed out his robe. His eyes were agleam. The time for daintiness was fast drawing to a close, he thought. This was going to be a truly remarkable experience.

He rolled over onto his abdomen. He put a large white Egyptian cotton towel over his buttocks and spread a generous amount of flower scented lotion on his back. He was well built and muscular. He did not have a hair on his back or under his armpits, having hand plucked his own axillary hair and had a Brazilian wax job on his back.

She warmed some lotion in her strong hands, straddled him and began to knead and press his knotted back muscles. He began to relax. He squirmed enough to know that lying on his abdomen was growing increasingly uncomfortable due to changes occurring related to the pleasure he was experiencing.

She gingerly slid her left hand under the pillow and found the knife taking care not to cut herself.

"Why don't you turn over on your back, dear Daud; I think you would be more comfortable that way."

He did so, still feeling a little shy about the degree of his enthusiasm for the massage. She adjusted the towel over his growing enthusiasm and straddled his chest.

"Put your hands behind your neck, and relax. This should be a very nice feeling."

She leaned over to give him more of an eyeful than any other man than her husband had ever seen.

"Close your eyes. Let my hands take you to *Jannah* [Paradise]," she said caressing him with both her voice and her hands.

He found himself becoming so relaxed that he felt almost hypnotized. He was tired from his long day of giving speeches and seeking donations. He nodded off a little. It was quite wonderful—such nice hands, such a nice voice.

Sybil continued to massage his chest with her left hand and swiped the ceramic knife swiftly and deeply across his exposed throat. His carotid arteries, jugular veins, and trachea were all transected with that single stroke. He could not make a sound. He bled to death in less than half a minute. Sybil's legs were soaked in blood. The net stockings and garter belt were ruined. When she was certain that his death throes were done, she used the towel to get rid of the majority of the blood on her and ran to the bathroom for a quick shower. She inspected herself and saw no traces of Daud's life force on her.

Chapter Fourteen

She glanced at her watch. She had been in the bedroom for just under ten minutes. She stripped off the rest of her underclothes, which had escaped the blood, and wrapped them and the knife in the towel. She switched towels in the bathroom; so, she would not take any risks of dripping his blood on the hallway carpets thereby leaving a telltale trail. She wrapped the brunette wig in the towel with the sexy underclothes and placed it in an empty plastic garbage sack.

Time was ticking away. Either the family would return, or the guards would become curious. She could not possibly walk nonchalantly out the door and down the hall to peace and freedom before the thugs found Daud's body and came out howling for her blood. What to do?

As she searched aimlessly around the bedroom for a way out of her predicament, she noticed six USB flash drives lying on the bedside table. On impulse, she scooped them up and shoved them into her purse. You never knew when something like that would come in handy. She wracked her brain for something clever to do, but gave up. She would either brazen it out and outrun them when the guards found Daud, or she would have to do something drastic. She had the training and plenty of newly hatched skills. She elected to go the tough-guy route.

She undid her garbage bag collection and removed the knife. She left the wrapped garbage on a chair and walked to the bedroom door. She looked into the sitting room. All clear. She moved to the closed apartment door. She opened it tentatively and caught the eye of one of the guards. She was improvising second by second. She backed up into the room and silently beckoned the guard with a waggling of her crooked index finger. He gave her a quizzical look but followed her in.

137

Sybil moved a little faster to create space between herself and the guard. The room was pitch dark, and she had the advantage of having adjusted to the darkness before summoning him. He walked forward into the room extending his arms to avoid a collision with furniture and moved about trying to find a light switch. Sybil stood to his left side— his weak side—and before he could flip the wall switch, she swiped the razor-blade sharp edge of the ceramic knife across his throat. His carotid was cut, and he clasped his hands to his throat in a futile attempt to stop the gushing torrent of blood. Sybil stood back in the darkness to avoid any lucky blow from him and from the blood spatter that was sure to be extending out several feet.

The guard toppled over, his fight with the Grim Reaper at an end. Sybil waited until it was quiet, and she could no longer hear his violent attempts to breathe and to strike out. She turned on a small table lamp. The guard was face down on the floor. His hand was on his gun. That posed a problem. She had to turn him over to get the gun, but to do so would get blood all over her. She ran to the bathroom and pulled off a towel rack. She used the metal rack as a pry bar and turned him over. She extracted the gun from its holster, and was infused with a renewal of hope when she realized that the gun had a baffle suppressor. If she had to shoot, she at least would not make a big racket which would draw in outsiders.

She heard the second guard calling from the sitting room, "Muhammad, what's going on, brother? You still in the bedroom? What's up?"

He was speaking Arabic which Sybil understood clearly.

Improvising again, she called out, "Guard, come in here, quick. Something's wrong."

That she called to him in Arabic was confusing, and he entered the darkened bedroom with his gun drawn but unsure what was happening.

Sybil had the distinct advantage that he was looking forward into darkness, and she could see his silhouette against the glow from the lamps in the sitting room. She aimed at his chest and fired two shots that sounded like 'splut, splut' instead of a large bang. He started his fall to the floor, but as he did, he got off one round.

The 9 mm slug ripped a hole through Sybil's dress and angled through and through her left flank. It surprised her. The pain was instantaneous and terrible—a nightmarish stinging sensation like a hive full of killer bees had landed on that spot. She turned on the bedside lamp and was dismayed to see blood beginning to seep out quite quickly. It did not seem to be spurting; so, she presumed that the bullet had cut through a fairly large vein. She began to feel faint and light-headed. She knew that she had not lost that much blood, but she was going into shock anyway. Her thinking was proceeding as if the electrochemical impulses had to travel through thick insulation. She had the wits to pick up her trash bundle and her purse with the flash drives in it and to head for the door.

There was no one in the hall. She wanted to head for the stairwell, but it was fifty yards away. It looked like a mile. Her vision began to fade, to close in on her. Her motor function was failing and her finger jerked firing off a round which hit the wall across from Daud's suite harmlessly. She had enough mental function to curse herself and to see that she was now seriously bleeding. She fell face forward on the floor, and everything faded to black.

The accidental firing of the pistol saved her life. The bullet cut its way through the wall in the suite across the hall where Ed and his men were waiting on tenterhooks because Sybil had been too long in the room with the terrorist. They flew out of the door and found her on the floor with blood beginning to pool on the carpet by her hip. Ed stayed with her and pressed his hand hard down onto the wound. The two other CIA agents raced into the dark apartment. In a few seconds, the three Company men assessed what had gone on and moved smoothly into action.

Ten minutes later, a clean-up team from Paris CIA headquarters arrived without anyone in the hotel being the wiser. EMTs took care of Sybil and rushed her to the headquarters clinic where the bleeding was controlled. IV saline and 0.1 mg of epinephrine brought her blood pressure back up and got blood flowing to her brain again. The cleaners removed the blood in the hallway carpet; they were efficient experts with years of experience. They collected Sybil's purse and the garbage bag with the bloody towels and underwear. They dropped the blood covered knife on the bed to convince the French cops that the three dead men had killed each other, and there was no particular reason to extend the investigation further afield.

When the CIA team cleared the area, there was no sign of anything wrong in the hall, but the bedroom was a crime scene that would not take much in the way of mental gymnastics for the Sûreté to conclude that there had been an internecine fight. The obvious conclusion was that one guard cut his boss's throat and shot the other guard when he discovered the murder in progress. The second—innocent—guard was able to get off a lucky shot that killed the murderer before he died.

Sybil was flown home to recuperate, but was up and around the second day back. She was released from Walter Reed Hospital in good health but WITH a sore side. The most difficult part of the entire episode came when she had to explain to Charles what had happened. He learned only that she had been a hero; that came from DDCIA who felt like Charles deserved that much. Sybil was given another award, this time the second highest the intelligence service had to offer—the Intelligence Star.

Of course, it had to remain secret. Sybil accepted both the medal and the secrecy with grace. Charles had only one thing to say to his incredible wife.

"My dear, your life is pretty much a tangle of secrets and scandals. I am taking you home. What's next?"

-The End-

Sybil Norcroft Book Four

Secrets and Scandals

In this, the 4th in the Sybil series, Sybil is given an ultra-top-secret clearance rating based on her previous performance and her ice-in-the-veins way of going about the Company's business. Now she has to juggle life as a wife and mother keeping secrets, as a famous public figure in her profession as a network medical consultant news reporter, and as a CIA agent who is under threat of assassination from an unseen and unnamed mole in the intelligence community. When three of her fellow agents are murdered, Sybil is offered the job of finding the mole which considerably increases her chances of meeting harm. What she does will involve secrets and scandals at the highest level of government.